S0-CBY-027

Penguin Books
Grey's Valley

Hugh Atkinson was born in country New South Wales in 1924. He has lived and travelled in many countries and has worked as a journalist, scriptwriter, copywriter, radiowriter, and as special war correspondent for the London *Sunday Telegraph* – an experience from which he wrote the celebrated *Most Savage Animal* (1972).

Since his first novel, *The Pink and the Brown,* was published in 1957 Hugh Atkinson has become one of Australia's few internationally published authors, with many translations, prizes and films to his credit. He is probably best known for *The Games* (1967), which appeared in ten languages, won the American Literary Guild Prize, and was filmed by 20th Century Fox.

Hugh Atkinson is currently living and writing in 'the drop-out country' in New South Wales.

Also by Hugh Atkinson

The Pink and the Brown (1957)
Low Company (1961)
The Reckoning (1965, and 1977 as *Weekend of Shadows*)
The Games (1967)
Johnny Horns (1971)
The Most Savage Animal (1972)
The Man in the Middle (1973)
Crack-Up (1974)
Unscheduled Flight (1976)
The Manipulators (1978)
The Pyjama Girl Case (as Hugh Geddes, 1978)
Billy Two Toes' Rainbow (1982)
The Longest Wire (1982)

a novel by
Hugh Atkinson

GREY'S VALLEY
The Legend

Penguin Books

Penguin Books Australia Ltd,
487 Maroondah Highway, P.O. Box 257
Ringwood, Victoria 3134, Australia
Penguin Books Ltd,
Harmondsworth, Middlesex, England
Penguin Books,
40 West 23rd Street, New York, N.Y. 10010, U.S.A.
Penguin Books Canada Limited,
2801 John Street, Markham, Ontario, Canada L3R 1B4
Penguin Books (N.Z.) Ltd,
182-190 Wairau Road, Auckland 10, New Zealand

First published by Penguin Books Australia, 1986

Copyright © Hugh Atkinson, 1986

All Rights Reserved. Without limiting the rights under copyright reserved
above, no part of this publication may be reproduced, stored in or introduced
into a retrieval system, or transmitted, in any form or by any means
(electronic, mechanical, photocopying, recording or otherwise), without
the prior written permission of both the copyright owner and the above
publisher of this book.

Typeset in Baskerville Roman by
Leader Composition Pty Ltd, Melbourne
Made and printed in Australia by
The Dominion Press – Hedges & Bell, Victoria

CIP

Atkinson, Hugh, 1924- .
Grey's Valley.

ISBN 0 14 009394 X.

I. Title.

A823'.3

To Viola and being reborn

If you are in those hills you will be taken to the valley and told this story.

In the early days of the colony Alec Grey took passage out of Liverpool on a four-masted barque and sailed as an immigrant for Australia. He wasn't transported, he was his own free man and skilled with the saw and the hammer. They say that he was a big man and that the twins grew up to be like him. They say, out of the stories, that Alec Grey wore a black beard that covered his chest and that he was like a great polished rock in his purpose and as inflexible as a rock and terrifyingly righteous.

Alec Grey went ashore in Sydney and took the saw and the hammer. He did not mind the drunken soldiers and paid scant attention to the convicts. He did not mind the pale indifference of the landscape in which there would have been no reference to anything he had known.

They guessed, the old ones who had first told it, and had known Alec Grey in the valley, that he would have laboured with his tools to help build the troubled young settlement on the blue water, among the gum trees.

He would have laboured as he did in the valley, to realise the making that must have been in his mind. Perhaps that making had always been in his mind and he had needed to ship out of Liverpool to a new country. A new country where a man could take up land, if his need for land was severe enough.

It is said that he married in that time and that his wife was

1

a bonded woman. Nobody knew properly about that until many years afterwards. There was a tin-type of Alec Grey's wife on a wall of the house in the valley. She looked pale, frail and frightened in the tin-type, clasped hands in her lap and a cameo brooch pinned to the high neck of her sombre dress.

Others had crossed the mountains leaving tracks to follow. Blaxland, Wentworth and Lawson had found a way over the blue barrier that had pinned the settlers to the coast. Mile upon mile of tumbled precipice and peak, the deep rips and chasms and impossible escarpments. They found a way across, climbing from one tall spine to another, which they could see had the hope of going in the wanted direction.

The explorers laboured their horses and themselves up one spur and another, to be turned back yet again on the edge of some awesome drop. At which in distant ages the bottom had dropped out of the ranges, but they kept to the spines and they found a way across.

They found a way across the hazy blue and came down on the other side, into foothills and folded valleys and rushes of verdant soil and grass. Water ran on the other side, more creeks than rivers, but there were rivers, good ones, further out on the plains.

They turned back when they got the plains, full of the wonder of grazing country. Grazing country enough, it seemed, to feed all the sheep and cattle in the world. They backtracked their passage, following the trees they had blazed with axes, and got back to describe the plains and the grass and the rivers, the inland of the colony which had been no more than a thousand conjectures.

The settlers had something to wonder at and stilled their impatience until some form of road would be built. They couldn't follow the explorers with drays and waggons. Not up and down the slippery spurs and in detours around chasms where the bottom had fallen out of the world.

They had to await some form of road, which the govern-

2

ment surveyor would build with convicts to do the work, the road or track across the mountains to the plains.

That thread of road across the mountains would lead to the settling of a state. The oldest continent, which had been there in a dream like the Aborigines' stories of their Dreamtime. There were those who were fated when the explorers brought the news. Fated to be the pioneers, fated to be the landtakers. Fated to found empires built on grass, driving their flocks before them.

Fated for heartbreak and ruin in the droughts, when winds with mouths like furnaces shrivelled the grass they had built on, blew it away, and the sheep and the cattle and the horses parched and skeletoned and died.

The road across the mountains was being trafficked when Alec Grey went ashore. There were bullock carts and drays and waggons on it, and those who walked pushing their possessions in barrows. The stage-coaches of Cobb and Co. were carrying passengers across the mountains, which required as much stamina from those in the coaches as it did from the harnessed teams.

There were settlements growing on the plains with names being given to them. Bark shanties selling flour and salt and sugar, treacle and cloth, weapons and ammunition, wideawake hats and moleskin trousers. There were tents selling grog, boots, tobacco, saddles and harness.

The grass of the plains was being grazed on by four-legged things which flabbergasted the Aborigines when they saw them. More than flabbergasted them when they saw a man on a horse dismount, because how could such an unthinkable animal divide into two living parts.

They say that when Alec Grey had earned enough he outfitted a dray and pack-horses. He had a single furrow plough on the cart. The building tools were in the brass-bound box he had brought from Liverpool. He had a keg of beef in brine on the cart and the brine made noises sloshing about. He had packed all he would need for his purpose, including the wife who sat beside him on the plank that

3

served for a seat on the dray. You needed a wife to do what Alec Grey would do, someone to work beside him in the necessary gender to breed by.

The lift of the ranges bore his small caravan higher, Alec and his wife higher and higher, where the air thinned and cooled and a man did not sweat if he had to put his shoulder to the wheel to heave the cart out of a rut, or out of a bog if it rained the way it could in the mountains, bringing wisping and curling wraps of fog.

When the fog concentrated it was as much as you could do to make out the heads of the horses. When camp was made beside the road a throw-out of canvas was needed. The canvas would squelch under a body and the blankets would need wringing out in the morning.

What we don't know and were never told was what Mary Grey might have been thinking. That pale, frail, frightened looking woman in the tin-type. If she had been a bonded woman she must have been transported. If she had she must have been young at the time, because she wasn't old in the tin-type. You could be transported, and there were those who had been, for the stealing of a loaf of bread. What might Mary have been thinking on this new road in an unknown country, lurching painfully on a dray with Alec Grey beside her?

Did she love Alec Grey? Did Alec Grey love her? Or did he, the inflexible rock with a black beard across his chest, represent to Mary the only escape she had been offered after the woman's prison? The most you could hope for, if you had been bonded, was marriage. Or prostitution in the rum-drunk stews of the colony, or being the slave of a free settler or ticket-of-leave man.

We don't know what Mary might have been feeling and thinking on the dray. They said, the old ones who knew her afterwards, that she kept to herself when there were visitors in the house. She would serve them tea from a set of china, and slices of brownie cake and fruit cake. Her husband sat at the head of the table, which he had cut out of

4

cedar. There would be a lace-edge cloth on the table, which Mary had sewn. Her husband sat in a high-backed chair which he had made out of cedar, one in a set of four. Four chairs at the table were all that would be needed in the house. One for Alec, one for Mary, and one each for the twins when that time came.

They say that Alec Grey had his mind resolved before he left Liverpool. He must have done, because he brought the apple seeds with him. Shiny brown and pointed seeds, each with a tree inside it. A tree that would grow apples and go on doing it until it had to die. Seeds that Alec had got somewhere in England, that had travelled with him halfway down the world and across the mountains and down the other side.

They were not ordinary apple seeds; they must have been from a particular strain, because fifty years afterwards there were no other apples to compare with the Grey's. Grey's Apples had long been famous in the Sydney markets by then. Those seeds must have contained a passion to grow, and wherever they had come from they couldn't have been fussy or fretful at being taken halfway down the world.

Those seeds were as compelled to grow as Alec Grey was compelled to plant them, in any soil with nourishment in it and moisture enough to soften and crack their shiny brown carapaces. To let out the adventure, with roots in its memory and a trunk and branches and leaves and fruit in its memory. Fruit enough to try the branches with their weight and to bend the lighter branches almost double.

Going back into the oldest stories, there is nothing said about Grey's Apples ever having sickened, getting spots and blotches on them and being no good. There were others who said that it wasn't because of something in the seeds. It was something in the valley. It hadn't been in the seeds not to sicken. It had been in the valley not to let them sicken.

Alec Grey could have known that there was something in

the seeds. He could have kept it in mind during the windblown months and the months of being salt-sprayed and the months of flapping canvas, when it must have seemed that the world had run out of land. A man can have seeds in his mind as well as in his pocket, or wherever Alec Grey had carried those seeds.

It's hard to know, when a man takes up land, how much in the end is owed to his making and how much is owed to the land. There are good seeds and bad seeds, and good and bad land, and sometimes land like Grey's valley.

It's hard to think of that valley as land. It's hard not to think of it as a person, or some inert animal, present but remote, with a life in it so distant that it can only be sensed by sparks in the brain that expire with such rapidity that they might never have lit.

It's hard to believe that the valley had not waited. Why had it arranged a spring at its head that drought or flood never altered? With volcanic soil in it and precious little anywhere else. With a stand of cedar above the spring, good red cedar that grew in the pattern of a half-circle as though for a benediction. What was the cedar doing there if not for Alec Grey and his axe and saw and hammer? What was the volcanic soil doing in that one fold of the foothills, with a spring at its head, the cedar for the timbers of a house and a table and four chairs and the rooms that Alec Grey built out of the cedar?

The road or track over the mountains, from which the eucalypts had been carved back, passed the narrow entry to the valley. Many had used that road without looking to the valley. In spite of the fact that a narrow bridge had been built where the spring ran out of the valley and had cut deep into friable soil so that a bridge had to be built.

The convicts had built it, a hump-backed bridge of granite, patterned on something English, or Roman, which the English had patterned on. The convict bridge was convex in the belly and the last exuberance of the spring that had cut there petered out in another mile.

There had been waggons and carts and men on horseback who had crossed the hump-backed bridge. There had been men freighting supplies to the plains. Nobody had looked to the spring that had been the reason for the bridge. The spring that had to come from somewhere, and had come from high up in a valley.

Alec Grey could have known that there was something he must look for. An idea of something, or a haunt of something he must look for. He might have been turning his head and looking all the way across the mountains. He had got himself a dray and pack-horses, provisions and a wife; the seeds were in a leather pouch tied at the top. He could have known that he had an appointment, one that would fill all his remaining days, and that he would not fail to recognise it when he saw it.

When Alec Grey reached the hump-backed bridge he must have reined in and stopped. He must have looked beyond the bridge to search out the mouth of the valley. He must have trod towards it, seeing the spring and looking up to the cedars, squatting to take up handfuls of the soil and letting it run through his fingers.

If he had carried in his mind from Liverpool the idea of an appointment, he would probably have said a prayer, because Alec Grey was terrifyingly righteous.

Before a sharp-pointed apple seed could do the things in its memory, Alec must have known the environment it would need. In the upper half of the valley, before it got to the spring, there was sunlight in the mornings. In the heat of the day one wing of the valley cast a mantling shadow. There would be frosts in winter and the apple seeds had memories of English frosts.

Alec Grey would have first done what every landtaker had to do. Put up a tent to live in and break ground for a kitchen garden. The first planting and growing is always for survival. Root vegetables, such as potato and carrot. Beans for something green. Onions for health. There would have been meat enough in the keg of brine.

He would have made bush beds to go in the tent. With forked branches cut to the proper length, four of them to a bed, two at each end. With two saplings to be pushed through the sides of the hessian bags, the bags that would have carried hard feed for the horses, and fit the saplings into the forks.

Only when those tasks had been completed would he have had the time to go up the valley and site the orchard. He might have had it in his mind, but there would have been other things to look to. Rocks to be broken up or removed, dead wood to be burned off and gums to be felled and their roots dug out. There would have been many months of labour before a horse was harnessed to the plough. His bright, new plough, the wooden handles clean of sweat-stain. When the furrows had been curled there would still be the harrowing to do. And many small snaking roots to be hauled out of the earth. His first ploughing and harrowing would have been left to breathe, while he made a nursery for the apple seeds and waited on the sprouts, to be transplanted up the valley.

Seeds have their own time. Alec Grey would have known that it would be ten years or more before apples came to the orchard. The rows he had planted would be in leaf before then, rustling and scraping on each other, sibilant when winds tousled among them.

In that time he could go to the cedars with his axe, lop the trunks of their branches and put a horse to hauling the trunks to where he would work them. He would split the trunks with wedges into sweet-smelling planks, red when the sap is in them, patterned in arboreal rings. In the years of being seasoned the planks would change colour but they would continue to give out a faint good smell.

He had to wait on the cedar to season and he had to wait on the trees to fruit, but he did not have to wait on his house. The house he and his wife would one day live in would be half granite and half cedar and he did not have to wait on the granite. The granite blocks would go up out of a granite foundation and that would be work enough while the elements seasoned the cedar.

Cedar beams would be positioned for the roof, with three-inch nails to be hammered in securing the galvanised iron. Which he might have got out of a trade, if galvanised iron was being hauled over the hump-backed bridge, or he might have journeyed for it in the dray to where the iron could be got. Cooking would have been done in the round-bellied cast-iron pot, suspended above the granite fireplace outside the tent. Or the damper bread could have been baked in scoops of hot embers, the burning ash and embers put back over the damper.

It is known that Alec Grey broke new ground beneath the orchard and planted there, for corn cakes to eat and grain to strengthen the horses, grain to trade with those who never stopped coming down from the mountains. The spring made water enough to be independent of the seasons and trenches were dug to irrigate the grain. The violent wind storms never troubled Alec Grey's corn. The cedars, which were of the valley but not in it, standing in their half circle like a grave conference of priests, broke the winds, leaving only tatters to be taken down the valley.

Grey's valley, the long and secret fold, was abundant in its blessings. And perhaps overblessed and someone had to pay for it one day.

Where the spring got up there was a shelf of granite around it, slivers of granite with earth and moss on them, poking out of the cover like teeth. There was a marsh there with many leeches in it. The migratory birds knew the spring and the marsh and arrived there in their seasons in brilliantly coloured flocks. The wild duck also knew that place and when they came flapping in to settle, Alec Grey could get any number with the gun.

Mary Grey must have toiled as did her husband. Makings were not easy then and more often followed by heartbreak and ruin than they were by success. It was different in Grey's valley and those who came to know it often went

9

bitter-eyed with envy, and bitter-tongued with envy, and gave Alec Grey little credit for his back-breaking labours. Considering what he did there, with not many years to get it done, with never a man to help him, one can believe that he must have worked by moonlight.

The house he had started was a big imagining. He didn't wait for years to get established and then get a house built. He started on that house while he was still waiting for the cedar to season and waiting for the orchard to fruit. The house in his mind was a big one, built to last forever, built for a big family.

Before he left Sydney in his dray, with the four pack-horses, he must have worked at making lists of everything he would need. There must have been many things strange to him which he would have had to learn. There is no evidence that he had ever grown apples or corn, and most certainly had not cut cedar or built a house of mountain granite and cedar. He must have put everything that he knew he would need on his lists. How did he know he would need a seven-pound hammer to work granite and the wedges to do it? He might have known that he would need an adze to shape timber and a chain for logs which a horse could pull if he had the right harness. He might have known that he would need spare boots for man and wife, when those on their feet fell apart. How did he know he would find a place to plant sharp-pointed apple seeds? With a spring in its head that never failed and a priestly conglomeration of cedars? And the volcanic soil with the urgency in it to accelerate anything planted?

Mary Grey must have had her own lists to make. Calico to patch clothing, stout thread and needles, scissors and a measuring tape for the making of new clothes from bolts of cloth. Liniments for cuts and sprains, castor oil for the stomach, herbal medicines for fevers. And perhaps something treasured and put away for the time to wear it. Something pretty put away with beads and a bangle.

10

Alec Grey would have got a cow and Mary would have milked it and churned butter when the cream was good. He would have got a ram and ewes and waited on the ewes to lamb. There would have been fresh mutton then and pickled mutton, mutton enough to trade at the hump-backed bridge with those who continued to come down in anything with wheels they could ride on. There would have been luck in his trading with those who could not, or would not, go any further – out of disasters that had happened, or a failure of courage – and they would trade off things they had put on their lists to get back over the mountains.

The track had been hard trod and wheeled by then and word had got back that trade could be done near the hump-backed bridge. A strong man handy with tools could replace floorboards in waggons and carts. He could lift a laden cart single-handed, if a new wheel had to be fitted. He had a valley nearby and was growing apples in it and you couldn't see much of his face because of the black beard. Mary Grey must sometimes have seen other women when a transport had to stop for repairs. If there was a woman she might have been sent to the valley to drink tea and have something to eat.

It is known that in the time when the house was getting ready to be lived in, Mary Grey had a child. It had been a girl and had lived for a year. There was a granite marker for it on a knoll near the house. The dates of birth and death were chiselled on the marker. The name given to the child had been Elizabeth. There might have been an Elizabeth in Mary's family, or in the family of her husband.

The child could have died of anything. There was whooping cough in the colony and it could have carried over the mountains. There were fevers, colds in the lungs, the pestilences flesh are heir to. Mary might not have had much milk in her breasts.

Alec Grey would have delivered the girl, with those great lumped and calloused hands that helped the ewes to lamb, the mares to foal, the bitches to whelp. The same hands –

11

almost the same – which would help deliver another Mary Grey, in the course of time, after both Alec and Mary had been put away on the knoll. The big house had long been built then, and the scatter of outbuildings around it.

Alec Grey would have known how to deliver the child out of his experience with animals. He delivered the child that died and in the years afterwards he delivered his twin sons. One to be named Alec, after himself, and one to be named Mathew. Mathew could have been named after a brother or father in the old country, or after a brother or father of Mary's.

When the girl child had been buried she had been put away in a cedar coffin made by her father. He had read over her from the family Bible, from which he read every night after supper no matter who might have been in the house. When the tiny coffin had been covered, Alec had dug the granite marker in so that it could not fall over.

Despite how a man might yearn for a son or a daughter, it must be different for the mother who has borne the child in her body. It would be hoped that Alec Grey gave Mary comfort, some source of solace; because out of the stories told there is little in them to give Alec a common humanity. There is always an awe of him, an awe of a brooding force that could not be stopped or altered. Despite the grace and blessings of the valley, it was believed that Alec would have wrestled with an ice flow, or with a desert, if that was where he had to do the things he had to do.

It is certain that those who knew him didn't venture far with Alec Grey. They would speak in a puzzled way about him and the valley. They might say that he wasn't easy to be at table with. He had too much silence in him and his eyes could make you uneasy. When he spoke it was seldom that he took up anything being said. He might say that he had new ground to break.

If a man was putting in crop he would ask about the seeds. Where had he got them and what did he know about the seeds. He might say that you couldn't tell about soil by looking at it. That you had to crumble it up on the skin of your hands, put your face into it and feel that it was good enough to eat. Get the soil into your nostrils before you could know about it.

In stories of the valley there are stories about his strength, and those who told about it were no weaklings. There is a piece recited about him which had gone into bush lore, although those who repeat it don't know that it had a living model. He was massive in the shoulders and arms, taller than others, and wider. And there were other tall and wide men at that time.

All that was said about Mary was that she was pretty. Perhaps she had chest trouble to make her so pale and thin. She kept her head down when she served at table.

It got about that Alec Grey must have a haunt in him, because he never stopped breaking ground. Fifteen years after he had come to the valley, he continued breaking new ground. The orchard was growing down the valley from where it had started. Below the grain field there was another orchard of citrus. The cedar stand had enlarged, encouraged in its re-shooting by Alec.

The valley became a haunt to others, its throat bulging with apples, the waist of the valley bulging with grain crops and citrus. It wasn't citrus country but the trees and fruit flourished. Passionfruit clambered over the outbuildings, great vines of it, and passionfruit was almost unkown. Nobody knew where those vines had come from or why they had wanted to grow in the valley.

Where the spring came up and made a marsh Alec had put in willow cuttings, the slim and beautiful droops of weeping willow. Those cuttings must have come from a river because willow needs a river, or water enough around them to make them think they have a river.

Alec Grey must have felled willow and given it time to season because there was a rocking chair of willow and a willow table in the house.

If you had business in the valley, because Alec Grey

13

wasn't a man to visit, the first thing you noticed when you neared the house was a perfume. A perfume you could sense not only in your nostrils, but on your tongue. It was the green and sappy smell of apples that had been stored in the empty rooms. The green smell of apples had mingled into the cedar, and perhaps into the granite.

When the time came to harvest the apples there were many intinerant workers in the valley. And some who were not itinerant, but of the district and down on their luck. When they climbed the ladders to reach through the leaves for the fruit, it's no wonder if their thoughts were bitter. It would have been easy to see from the ladders, the profusion of everything growing in the valley.

They could see up to where the spring rose, making a marsh about it. The ditches off the spring where it became a creek, which Alec Grey had dug to irrigate his citrus. It would have been hard and bitter to them if their land was being parched. More so, if they felt themselves to be failing, that the land and the seasons had beaten them.

All Alec Grey in his valley had to do was let it fall into his lap. Hire men down on their luck and ready to do anything, to pick and box his apples and citrus and harvest his grain. To pack the harvest on a waggon and drive it away.

In Sydney, the colony had taken on manners. There were bragging houses being built and owners in bragging carriages. There was bragging clothing for ladies and gentlemen. Those who had more need to brag, or more money to brag with, ordered their clothing from London.

The talk there was no longer about survival, or how many convicts the Governor might grant for labour. Or whether or not the creatures should be flogged, if they were lazy or trouble makers. The talk was about wool and grain prices in London. Australian wines and brandies that had won awards and gold medals in London.

There were many dressed in imported English clothing, drinking English port and smoking imported cigars. The Aborigines were no longer spoken about as a problem. The

Aborigines had cleared out, or had been cleared out, of the immediate environments. It would be well to remember how to handle the blacks if you thought about taking an interest in a property across the mountains.

On the other side, where the mountains dipped down to the plains in sugar-loaf hills and valleys, other things were talked about miles from the hump-backed bridge.

Alec Grey and his valley were talked about. The unfairness and the accident of his having come across the valley. The twin sons that had been born, which he had delivered himself, and were growing up as wild as dingoes the way they kept to themselves if strangers were about. Alec with the silence on him, those startling grey eyes that could look through a man, the black beard fit to be sheared.

Why did he keep his wife locked up in the valley? Only seen sometimes in town, sitting in the sulky while one of her boys bought something. She no better than a little scrap of a thing. Alec Grey thought himself too good for others. His wife too good for other women, his twins too good for other boys. He was the one who had had the luck and they wished they had had a half of it, coming across that valley by the accident of it being there.

They had heard in the district how Alec Grey would read from the Bible after supper. Those who had been there on business and had been invited to stay for a meal, said that he would stop at the slightest noise. He would stab at the noise with his eyes and the craggy nose that came out of the beard. His wife and the sons would listen, heads bent. The visitors would know that when the Bible was closed it was time for them to leave.

There was another story told by a farmer who did business with Alec Grey. He said that old Alec couldn't have had all that much Bible in him. Certainly nothing about turning the other cheek. He had been riding to see him about a matter of trade. There was a brokendown dray near the hump-backed bridge and he could see from the distance that there were four men around the dray and that

Alec Grey was there. One of the men must have fetched him. He would still come out for a breakdown, long after trade or money would have mattered.

The four men must have heard about Alec Grey's prosperity and been in need enough to plot to rob him. To get him out of the house on the pretext of a breakdown, so they could get back to the house.

He said that he could see from a distance that Alec was bending over a wheel. He saw one of the men use something to strike Alec on the head. He saw him stand up instead of being knocked senseless. He heard the roar that came out of him. He said that when he got to the bridge the four men were stetched out, two of them bloodied yards from the dray, two making no sound.

Alec Grey had picked up his hat. He took a grip of the bridle on the horse the farmer was riding. He said, 'We will go to the house.'

He made no mention of the four men, some of whom were getting up. The farmer made no mention. He asked how could you make a mention being led on the bridle by a man who had shut it out.

Other things had been growing, ten miles from the convict bridge. The hamlet had become a town with the Aboriginal name of Warrawang. It became important enough to have a siding on the rails that had come over the mountains. There wasn't much to the siding, other than a sign spelling out Warrawang.

A three-room bank in brick had been built. With the orchard in the valley always enlarging itself, as Alec Grey persisted in breaking new ground, there was an industry in the season getting Grey's Apples to the railway to be freighted to the markets.

In that season there were camps in the valley and fires at night. There was the sound of men singing and the music of concertinas and mouth organs. Sometimes angry shouts and fighting, if grog had been brought to the valley.

It must have been strange to Mary Grey, all that hullabaloo going on, shattering the peace of the valley. Mostly there would have been nothing to hear other than the voices of her family. The finches, diamond sparrows and redheads, in the hedges that had been planted, the screeching of parrots on the grain crops and the bleating of sheep.

There had been nothing like the noise of men during the years of the first making. When she had nursed a baby until it died and was buried on the knoll in a cedar coffin. She might have felt little fulfilment in all that had been made. She might have felt horror at last about a making that never stopped. That had to go on as though there never could be enough.

She might have waited on a different making, a making of peace and love. The way a simple woman can need a simple love.

Her heart might have swelled up and begun to die, worn out with the making. Worn out with respect for her strong unbending husband. And now the twins growing up in the image of their father, as though in his will he had produced them out of himself by cellular division, four more hands and four more legs to work his will in the valley.

Mary was talked about in the town, which could have been a way of getting back at her husband. A pretended or a proper pity went with it. She was never known to say a word for herself. Except when she was putting out tea and cake, or serving food at the table.

The valley was there to see, but only at a distance, because Alec Grey closed himself off to others. Unless they had business and were there on his terms, and if they stayed for supper he would read the Bible at them. Never once did he or his family attend a visiting time. When a wedding or a christening was being celebrated, or Christmas or Easter, or a stroke of good luck. Or when others might feel plain sociable, or solitary, and invite the neighbours from miles around. Not more than a dozen were known to have overnighted in the valley, and never a woman.

When men were in the valley for the pruning or harvesting, Alec Grey would be there. He would ride up on one of the cobs he had bought, with a good hat on his head and elastic-sided riding boots on his feet. He wouldn't nod or smile at his big twin sons, who did their work like the men.

There had been talk in the town when the twins were born. Or after they had been born, because the twins must have been six months of age before anyone knew it. Tom Cosgrove, who delivered a weekly order of supplies to the valley, was the first to tell it.

'You coulda knocked me down with a feather,' Tom said, 'Didn't even know the Missus was carryin'.'

There was a big box on a post at the entry to the valley. Tom Cosgrove would deliver supplies to the box. Sometimes he would walk up to the house, because he and Alec Grey seemed to get on. Tom was the only one in town familiar with the family. He wouldn't hear a bad word said about Alec.

Tom would say, 'You don't understand old Alec. He's mighty set in his ways, I'll give yer that. But Alec's his own man. Anything Alec takes it inter his head ter do, Alec gets her done. He gets her done without fear or favour. He's been a fair man ter me over the years. Loaned me a few quid when I was on the bones of me arse. The only time I got up his nose was payin' him back. I put a bit of interest ter it. That got up old Alec's nose. The idea of takin' interest.'

The town got to know from Tom Cosgrove that heirs had been born to the valley. There were outcries from some of the women and noddings from the men. There had been no midwife at the birth and no women to tend Mary after the birth. One birth was hard enough, let alone twins.

Delivered by her husband. Have you ever seen those hands? Not as much as an invitation to see the twins in their cribs. That Alec Grey was an old monster. If he was here at this minute, they would tell him so to his face. If he wasn't a monster, he was too big for his boots. Nobody in the district was good enough for him. Certainly none of the women

18

who should have been there for the birth.

There was more after the shock of the twins having been born. Nothing had been said about a christening. Alec Grey with his Bible and the twins not as much as christened. Not as much as a christening party. He was no better than a hypocrite, reading from the Bible every night. It got about, from some inventive source, that Alec Grey had been a priest himself, which was why he was so righteous. He had not needed another priest to christen the twins.

The circling stand of cedar later impressed the bank manager with the notion of a gathering of priests conferring blessing. The valley was like that in the minds of the town. It was of the district but not in it. There could have been something in Alec Grey's character that kept him aloof. There could have been a private communing in him too dense to share, a burden of communing which he could not lay down. There could have been something in his memory which he could not lay down, out of the life he had lived in England.

The topography of the valley, so distinct and removed from everything about it, could have been a sacred place to the Aborigines, who were gone from there when Alec came down out of the mountains. Every valley is a scar made in the landscape, no matter how sheltering and nourishing. Alec Grey could have had his scars and contributed them to the valley. The valley which was a scar in itself could have contributed to his.

It is certain that the valley was of the district but not in it, as were the Greys. The valley and the family could go out of mind to those who were nearest to them. Nobody knew what might be happening there, except in rumour and story. When the girl child was buried it wasn't known for a time. When the twins had been born that wasn't known for months.

The valley became a haunt more than anything else. Its presence was inescapable, as were the people in it. With both being seldom seen, except in the seasons of pruning and harvesting, their nearby presence was felt.

In other than those two seasons of activity, those who maintained a curiosity as to what might be happening in the valley would have to ask Tom Cosgrove. Out of season the Greys were only visible to Tom and he enjoyed the privilege of knowing that. Alec Grey would sometimes be seen in the town when he had business. He would exchange G'days if he was offered one but never initiated it.

There was something in his presence that had an effect on others. Not only because he was the Grey of Grey's valley, but in the bulk and the beard of him. The brooding silence of the man that could be felt as a palpable thing. Apart from the fact that it was known that he was the richest man in the district. Apart from the envy that it had been him who had come across the valley.

Tom couldn't get back to town quick enough when the next thing to happen in the valley had happened. Tom had been a bit shaken himself and had to get to the Railway Arms to tell it. He was aware of his importance as the carrier of the news. Aware of his importance as the witness.

Alec Grey had met him at the delivery box, before Tom could walk to the house. Tom said that he had been standing there when he stopped the horse. He had said, 'G'day, Alec.' Alec had said, 'G'Day.' Tom had remarked on what a good day it was, and cool with a breeze in it for that time of year. Alec had said it was a grey day. A grey and grey day for the valley. Tom had not understood that because as far as he could see and feel the day was a high blue. Driving out he had taken off his hat for the pleasure of the breeze.

Alec Grey had stood there. Tom had asked if he wanted him to carry the supplies to the house. 'We will both carry the supplies,' Alec Grey had said.

He and Alec Grey had walked to the house. Tom said that he was already feeling peculiar. Near the house, Alec Grey had stopped. He had looked up from the outbuildings to the citrus and the grain. He had lifted his head to look up to the orchard and where the spring got up, and to the cedars.

He had said, 'Mary died yesterday, Tom. Me and the twins have put her in a coffin. We'd be obliged if you would attend Mary's burial.'

The twins had been sitting silently at the table when they entered the house. They had been nineteen then and already grown. The boys had nodded to Tom, continuing to sit there. The eyes they had got from their father, which could look through a man, were clouded, but there were no tears in them. Alec had fetched a bottle of port and poured a glass for Tom.

Tom had said to the boys, 'I'm sorry.'

He didn't know what to say or do. The high blue of the day with a breeze in it had become dull and grey to him.

He had asked their father, 'What happened?'

'We don't know,' one of the boys had answered.

'She went to bed,' their father said. 'She said she felt worn out. Mary had been feeling worn out, lately. When we got back from the orchard, we found Mary dead.'

Tom had drunk the port and poured himself another. He said that he had felt peculiar in his stomach. He said that it had been hard not to look at the tin-type of Mary Grey on the wall. He said that it had been hard to meet their eyes with his.

'We've dug the hole,' Alec Grey had said. 'Take the coffin to the hole,' he had told the boys.

The boys had gone out, leaving Tom and Alec.

Tom Cosgrove said that he couldn't get his mind together. He didn't know what to say or do. He said that he should have known something when Alec met him at the box, because he was dressed in the dark suit he only wore to town. The twins were wearing suits when he got inside, dark suits such as their father wore, but Tom should have known something before that, when Alec had met him at the box.

'We dug the hole next to Elizabeth's grave,' old Alec had

said. 'I will chisel a marker tomorrow.'

He had looked up to the tin-type. He had pushed at the beard which had got caught under a lapel of his coat.

He had said, 'There is a time to be born, Tom.'

Tom had a cigarette behind his ear and got it and lit it.

'And there is a time to die,' old Alec said, and put those eyes in their startling white surrounds, the same eyes that the twins had in them, directly on Tom.

Tom said that the words and the eyes had made him feel that his own time had come.

Old Alec had stood up and got the Bible. The Bible had a place mark attached to it, a long dark ribbon. Alec Grey had opened the Bible at the place he had marked. He had read there silently and then he had asked, 'Are you ready, Tom?'

Alec Grey and the twins must have carpentered the cedar coffin during the night because it takes time to carpenter a coffin. The coffin was in the hole when Tom Cosgrove and Alec Grey got to the knoll. It only had the one marker on it then, the marker for the girl child. There were to be other markers there, chiselled on granite.

The boys were standing head bent over the hole, their hands folded before them. Tom said that a great sigh had come out of Alec when he looked down on the coffin and began to open the Bible. He had looked all about the valley before he began to read. He had looked to the stand of cedar whose timber was in the coffin and then he had begun to read.

Tom said that what Alec Grey had read from the Bible was about the valley and the shadow of death. Even though I walk in the valley of the shadow of death, I will fear no evil. Tom didn't know the Bible, but he remembered those words. The words struck him, Tom said, because there was a valley in them. He said that the words about the valley and the shadow of death curdled his stomach.

When old Alec had finished reading he had nodded at the boys, who picked up the shovels which had helped make the hole, the soil heaped from the digging of the hole, one at each side of the hole, to cover the coffin.

When that was done and nothing left of the hole other than a new earth over it, a tiny scar on its surrounds the way the valley itself was a scar, Alec Grey had closed the Bible and plodded away as though he wasn't walking on the earth, as though he was walking in it. Or it had seemed like that to Tom Cosgrove, who followed after him behind the twins.

When they got to the house and sat in the cedar chairs around the cedar table, with Mary Grey looking down from the tin-type seeming more alive in it because she was dead and buried, with the boys putting out fruit cake and their father pouring port, he had seemed to fill the room on his own, according to Tom Cosgrove.

Tom said that he hurried to get the port and the fruit cake over. He still felt peculiar about the valley in the Bible, and the shadow of death in it, which Alec Grey had read in his sonorous voice. Because of the way the valley folded there could be an echo in it. When the valley was busy with men every raised voice made an echo.

Tom said, when he got back to the Railway Arms, he could still hear old Alec's voice about the valley and the shadow of death, and fearing no evil, echoing in his head. That he needed to get drinks down to still the echo.

Tom had got more drinks down than were good for him, before those echoes stopped. They had not stopped forever, because they returned to him when other things to happen in the valley had happened. When it was heard in the town that Tom was drinking in the Railway Arms, that there had been a death and a burial in Grey's valley, that Mary Grey had gone to bed worn out and had never got up, every loafer in the town and those who had better things to do, got to the Railway Arms to hear Tom Cosgrove tell it.

There were other deliveries he should have made after meeting Alec Grey at the box. They were never made on that day, the way Mary Grey had been worn out and did not get up. Tom Cosgrove became drunk out of need to still the echoes about the valley of death. Tom, who got along with Alec Grey, and out of that had more importance in the town than he would have had, and prime in importance now because he had seen Mary Grey buried, had to be taken home.

Tom Cosgrove didn't get a sight of Alec Grey for months after his wife had been buried. If he walked to the house there appeared to be no life in it, although he could see the twins working up the valley. It surprised Tom to see the twins breaking new ground so soon after the death of their mother. The valley was bulging and had been bulging; you wouldn't think of a need to go on making more.

After Tom had witnessed the burial of Mary Grey and got back to the Railway Arms, it was supposed in the town that old Alec would become more invisible than ever. The contrary happened, old Alec would be more in town than anyone could remember. He would drive there in his sulky, get out and buy things. Mostly from hardware, pounds of nails or a new axe handle, a tin of kerosine. He would go to the bank and sit in the manager's office, being offered tots of whisky. The bank manager told the shire clerk that something had changed in old Alec. He had not shrunken in his body but something was gone from his presence. He didn't have so much silence and was easier to deal with. He made mentions about how Sydney had been when he had arrived on a sailing ship.

He might be feeling his age, the manager said. He had married late and had fathered late and he could be feeling his age. He had buried a wife and a daughter and that could make you feel your age.

The manager wondered why Alec had never left the valley. He and his wife had come out of the mountains from Sydney and stopped at the hump-backed bridge, which everyone knew about. You would have thought that at some time he would have taken his wife back to visit. Alec Grey and his wife must have made friends in Sydney, certainly someone in common when they had met and got married.

When he was first working the valley, planting it with apple seeds, any seeds he could get, and with four-legged things which were another kind of planting, because they grew up and multiplied in the ordinary of seeds, it would seem that Alec Grey might have planted himself.

The valley continued to be a puzzle. Anything could happen there, things had happened, and you would not know about it until afterwards. The women's concern for Mary in the years before she died, was mostly for the sake of gossip. Now the twins were useful to gossip about. How could those handsome young men endure being shut up in the valley? They must be in their twenties now. If they were in town they would go to the Railway Arms for a beer, and talk with others. But they never properly shared in the town.

It was known that they read a lot. For years parcels of books had been arriving, addressed to Alec Grey care of the bank. Years ago there had been regular deliveries of long brown envelopes, with a Government stamp in the bottom left corner, which Tom Cosgrove had worked out to be a correspondence course in education.

The longest memory could not recall one occasion of joy in the valley. There were annual dances in the woolshed on the Tweedie property. Easter was a good time in town, with church attendances on Palm Sunday. Something always happened at Christmas. If Alec Grey was such a man for the Bible, he should have known the admonishment to share one's miseries and joys.

He knew about a time to be born and a time to die and about the valley of the shadow of death. He knew man born of woman cometh like the wind and is cut down like a flower. Tom Cosgrove had heard him say that when his wife was buried.

Alec and the valley were kin to each other. Singular and remote and folded in and sufficient.

There were those who asked what good was Grey's valley to the Greys. They seemed to get no joy from its abundance, or no joy that had ever been communicated or shared. What had Mary Grey got out of her efforts, other than a buried baby and two boys delivered by her husband and already like smaller rocks off their father's rock, before she was too worn out to live.

Alec Grey could be like the cedars. They do not shoot up like larrikin gums that can make do with anything, soon get it over and begin again. The lifetime of cedar can be twenty times that of paper bark and scribbly bark, white gum and yellow box. Cedar can be massive in the trunk, the way Alec Grey was massive. He might have been kin to the valley and everything in it and feel no need to explain himself, or be understood by others. If that old Grey had ever got joy from the valley, he had kept it to himself.

If he had waited on the valley, shipping out of Liverpool to find it, the valley could have waited on him. The valley could have had an obsession of its own and had waited on an obsessed man. It might have wanted the girl and her mother buried in it and Alec Grey in it, leaving two sons to do the remainder of its work. The valley could have had it in mind to get all that done and then make it wither away and return to its dreaming.

Old Alec continued to surprise the townspeople by his visits. Talking business and talking no business at all in the bank manager's office, and going off to the shops. If he was on the footpath he might say that it had been an early season, and mention the cross-cut saw he had bought.

He had eased out of hard labour after the death of his wife. The great muscles on him began to gentle and sag. He could make two in bulk of other men when that began to happen. When Tom Cosgrove made a delivery he always took tea and fruit cake with Alec now. Tom said that you couldn't tell the fruit cake from the ones Mary Grey used to make. He supposed that one of the twins must have learned the recipe.

He said that old Alec mostly pottered in the rose garden his wife had made. That he had been adding to the roses. Tom often took home bunches of red roses and yellow roses, blooms in pink and white. When the roses were blooming, Tom said, you could smell them before you got to the house. There would be two perfumes then, the roses and the apples. He often took eggs home. There had always been fowls in the valley but there were many more now. It looked as though Alec had been adding to the fowls. There were brilliantly coloured bantams, which were only good for looking at, because a dozen bantam eggs in a pan didn't make a big omelette.

The bank manager got to know about the roses and eggs. Old Alec had begun taking him gifts. The manager had always been careful with Alec Grey, not only because of his account, but because of the pressure that seemed to come out of him. When he got eggs and roses he could only conclude that Alec Grey was feeling his age.

The station master was another to be taken aback by eggs and roses. In the time of harvesting and freighting old Alec still kept an eye on things. He wasn't the way he had been about it. It was more as though he needed an excuse to get out of the valley.

'He's a funny old bugger,' the station master said. 'Sometimes he can't get a word out for minutes. He looks about him like he hasn't seen the station, him that's been coming here for years. With a box of eggs under his arm and a bloody great fist full of roses, like he's getting ready to propose.'

When the twins went to the Railway Arms there would be farm hands and stock hands drinking. Railway fettlers, if they were about, road gangs repairing culverts, fence builders and dam sinkers. Everyone noticed the twins when they entered because you had to notice two big men who were the spitting image of each other. The locals would tell those passing through that the Grey twins had just come in. That the family was the richest one thereabouts, and they

27

had a valley that was something to see.

The local loafers would try to butter up to the twins, to get invited to the valley. Or at least to ask questions about it. They had been brought up on stories about Grey's valley and stories about the twins' old man.

What interested the local girls was hearing it said that old man Grey could buy up any property in the district, if he had a mind to do it. He was getting on now and soon the twins would own it all.

That was beside the fact that the Grey twins were handsome enough to turn any girl's head. They didn't skylark about trying to impress the girls, which was what the girls were accustomed to. They stood upright and walked and talked that way, with a pride in their bearing. If the girls thought up an excuse to stop them in the street the twins were always polite.

The girls' best pretext was to ask the twins which was Alec and which was Mathew. Then they could squirm and giggle, touch their hair and jostle each other. They could say, 'You're as alike as two peas in a pod. If one of you walked out with a girl she'd never know which was which. Wouldn't know if you changed about, who was flirting with her.'

The twins would smile and say, 'I'm Alec.' Or, 'I'm Mathew.' If it was Mathew he would say, 'You can tell Alec, he's the old one. Alec was born twenty minutes before me.'

The twins weren't self-conscious if girls stopped them, but always polite, though nevertheless remote. Two young men who had never known a woman in any intimacy other than their mother, and had only been introduced to other women if they were the wife of someone who had come to the valley on business, never agonised or tried to show off, if pretty girls should stop them. They were remote in their manners, the way their father had been remote in the silence he had worn.

The married women in the town made opportunities to stop the twins. To peck at them with their eyes the way fowl peck in a fowl yard, and hope to get something out of them that could be turned into comment or gossip.

They might say to another woman who had a daughter:

'That Jeanie of yours must be going on nineteen. One of the twins would be a catch for Jeanie. You don't notice her bad eye when you get used to it. You've got to give it to her she's got beautiful hair. Yours must have been like that. Wouldn't do you and Mick any harm if Jeanie could catch one of the twins. When the old man dies it wouldn't be a hardship if you and Mick had to move to the valley.'

They might say:

'The Lord alone knows how they were brought up. That old miser for a father that locked up his wife in the valley. You've got to admit they've got manners. Ever notice their eyes? Grey eyes, with black lashes. Whites to them like the white of an egg when you fry it.'

Tom Cosgrove would often be included in the plotting:

'Tom's got that old miser's confidence. Tom knows the boys. Tom was there when the mother was buried. Why don't you fix it with Tom to get the boys invited home? They wouldn't have eaten home cooking since poor Mary Grey died. Not that I knew her to speak to. Used to see her in the sulky.'

The things that had always been said about Alec Grey had their seasons of repetitions. How he had got the valley by trampling over others. And wilder: he had been one of the last of the convicts and had come out on the ball and chain. The things he had done to get the valley could keep you awake at night. There had been no midwife when the twins were born. The old miser had been too mean.

The three Grey men visited the town together, which never before had happened. The two Alecs rode in the sulky and Mathew followed on horseback. That was enough to get attention from those on the streets. It was wondered what had brought them in, if there had been another happening in the valley. Interest was lost when they were seen to stop at the bank, that kind of interest.

The manager had a young teller who had come from Sydney to learn banking. He told his landlady where he boarded that he had been got to open accounts for the twins. Two deposit accounts and two cheque accounts. The twins could each draw on five hundred pounds.

That got about the town soon enough. There were not many in the town who had seen five hundred pounds at once. That two young men should have a cheque book to use and five hundred pounds to draw on, became a topic, particularly in the Railway Arms. Only a few Nobs in the town, and the owners of properties outside it, would ever have to use a cheque book.

The twins had always been different by being Greys. Now the other young men they talked with when they went to the bar, most of whom were doing as best they could at odd jobs and seasonal work, considered their disadvantages compared to the twins. Depending on character, they became fawning or kept apart, telling each other that the Grey twins knew where to stick the silver spoons they had been born with in their mouths.

Ma Baker, who had the boarding house with the young teller from the bank in it, and two loafing sons around the ages of the twins, had something to say when her sons went on about the cheque books the Greys had got. She said that the twins had the self-respect to get their hair cut and polish their boots. They carried handkerchiefs to blow in, instead of putting one thumb to a nostril and blowing snot out of the other. She wished to God that she might have had sons like that, silver spoons or not, instead of the loafing ne'er-do-wells that God had foisted on her.

The bank manager, who was a talker, said that he didn't know why old Alec had opened cheque accounts for the boys. After three months they had only drawn a few pounds between them. He had thought that they might be off to Sydney or had something important to buy.

He said that there had been something that bowled him over when one of the twins came in to collect a parcel of

30

books. When he was getting the parcel from the office he had asked the twin about the books they read.

'Mostly classics,' Alec, or Mathew, had answered. 'That's what Mum used to call them. Dickens, writers like that. We read all of Dickens. Poetry blokes like Lord Byron and Shelley, Henry Lawson and Rolf Boldrewood. Some of the plays of Shakespeare. Dad reckons we'd read anything with writing on it. Dad says we'd read the label on a bottle of hot sauce.'

The manager said that it had bowled him over. All he could remember of Dickens was having had to read him at school. The boys had grown up in the valley without ever having been to school.

The manager began to wonder about Mary Grey, if she had taught the twins to read and afterwards what to read. He had heard the rumoured story that Mary had been a bonded woman. He became curious about her and asked Tom Cosgrove what he knew. All that Tom had to say, was that she was real nice, the Missus. It seemed to niggle the bank manager that the Grey twins had read the classics.

In the routine of the following years nothing occurred in the valley worth talking about in the town. The town got bigger, with more weatherboard houses in it, a Church of England, this time a proper one, built in brick with arched windows and stained glass in the windows. The Grey twins would be seen in town, eight or ten times a year, making purchases of new shirts or boots and going afterwards to the Railway Arms. They would drink four beers when they visited, seldom more or less, and those who knew them knew that bad language offended the twins. They wouldn't complain or protest about it. If it was happening in their company one might look to the other, then they would finish their drinks and say, 'See you next time.'

The things said in the beginning continued to be said, if that was why the twins had left. 'Mealy mouthed bastards,' and, 'Bible thumpers like their old man.'

It didn't please those who felt put out, if there was a new

barmaid, particularly if she had come from out of town and was consequently untried, and could have been good for a bit of a poke. If she said, because of having been impressed by the twins, 'Dunyer know a gentleman when yer see one?'

The marriageable girls gave up. There was no point in stopping the twins on one pretext or another. All you could get out of them was a polite exchange. The marriageable girls who had set their caps for the twins, when the twins had been younger, were mostly married themselves now. They had married less dazzling prospects, having a bun in the oven.

In those years something else got into the stories about the Greys and the valley. A gentleman got off at the railway siding, or as much of a gentleman as anyone would admit, when you took in his clothes and the way he spoke. He wore a hard hat, curled on the brim, and a stick pin in his tie.

He walked from the railway to the Railway Arms and ordered a bottle of white wine. Vic Forbes, who owned the hotel, was working in the bar. He had no white wine, no wine of any colour. The stranger ordered whisky, not by the nip. He asked about the brands and had a bottle put out on the bar. He asked about accommodation for the night. There were a few rooms of accommodation.

There was a stock and station agent in the bar, doing business, and Tom Cosgrove who drank with the greengrocer. They slowed to inspect this new arrival. It was hard to get over a man dressed like that, with a ring on his finger.

'Passin' through?' Vic Forbes asked.

'I was through here thirty-five years ago. There was no town on the road then. I might have been on another road.'

Vic Forbes had trouble with thirty-five years ago. He would have been ten.

'Wouldn't have been many, that time.'

'That time,' the stranger said, 'there were those coming down on the mountain track, you couldn't put a mile between them.'

The others in the bar were listening, trying not to be

32

frank about it.

'Where were yer heading?' Vic Forbes asked.

'The gold fields. One of the many getting out to the gold fields.'

There were as many stories about the days of gold as there were about Grey's valley. Those in the bar let their own conversations die away.

'Any luck?' Vic asked, aware of the attention.

'No luck at Sunny Corner. Mostly alluvial gold. It was first come, first served, I wasn't one of the first.'

'Get to Trunkey?' Vic asked. He had heard about Trunkey.

'Trunkey and Sofala. You had to follow your luck.'

They had all heard about Sofala, where Hargreaves had found his nugget. Down the bar, and edging up, Tom Cosgrove said, 'Sounds like a Pom. Sounds a bit like old Alec.'

'Know about Hargreaves?' Vic asked, giving himself to the gold fields.

'I saw that nugget,' the arrival said, helping himself to the bottle.

'They reckon it was a big one,' Vic said.

'Up to yer belt buckle,' Tom Cosgrove said, forgetting himself.

The well-dressed man looked at Tom.

'That's right. There's a model of it in the Mineral Museum in Sydney.'

'Any luck?' Vic Forbes asked, looking again at the stick pin and the ring on the man's finger. All that had been many years ago. His customer didn't look it, but he could have been one of the old-timers.

'Ever heard of old crooked seam?' the arrival asked, pleased at this reception.

Tom Cosgrove had joined them now, delighted.

'I know about her,' Tom said. 'Heard about her from old Jim Bridges. Jumped about like a blue-bummed fly in a bottle.'

'That's right, friend,' the man said smiling. 'My partner and I bottomed on old crooked seam. Would you join me in a drink?'

It was learned that the man's name was Ben Saunders, when he introduced himself, offering to buy. There was more talk about the gold fields before he asked about Alec Grey.

Those in the bar joined the group with Ben Saunders, including the newcomers. There was nobody in the town who had known Alec Grey and the valley thirty-five years ago, before there was a town.

Ben Saunders shook his head when he learned about Mary Grey. About the twins big men now.

He told them more while they waited, their faces open to hear as much as they could. He told them that he had got the fever coming down from the mountains and was having delirium in his cart when Alec Grey had found him.

He had been nursed in the house by Mary Grey. She had given him medicines and put cold towels on his forehead and had read to him from Dickens. After Saunders and his partner had bottomed on old crooked seam, Ben had gone back to England. He said that when he had found himself getting on he had wanted to come back to see where it had all begun. He had wanted to see the old diggings. He said that he had never forgotten the Greys and had never forgotten that he had not gone back to thank them. When he had been able to travel again, Alec Grey had put supplies in his cart. He said that if it had not been for the Greys he might never have got to Sofala, to meet his Lady Luck.

They wanted to know what the valley had been like thirty-five years ago. Ben Saunders said he remembered the smell of apples and cedar in the house, and Alec Grey's questions about where he had come from in England. Ben had wanted to know about Alec Grey, but all that he had learned was that Alec's family was dead, or as Alec had put it, his family was dead to him.

He remembered the little girl's grave, up from the house.

Tom drove Ben Saunders to the valley next day, Tom groaning at the ruts and corrugations and swearing never to drink whisky again. He was to return and get him by three o'clock tomorrow, because there was a train for Bathurst at five which he wanted to be on. He wanted to take a look at what was left of Hill End. He and his partner had had enough luck at Hill End to set them up and keep them going.

Tom said that all that Ben Saunders would say about the visit, was that he would never forget it. He had mostly been silent on the drive back to town. Tom tried every way he could to learn where old Alec had come from, and why he had come from there. All that Ben Saunders would say, wearing his hard hat low on his forehead, was all that was over. It was over and had long been over, for Alec Grey.

There had been more drinking in the bar and an escort to the train for Ben Saunders. Tom Cosgrove was becoming drunk again and when he returned to the Railway Arms, got belligerent. He spoke about the mongrels who had never a good word for Alec Grey. Tom's mate, Ben Saunders, had come all the way from England to thank old Alec for keeping him alive. If there were any of those mongrels in the bar now, Tom announced, dashing his hat on the floor, they could put up their fists and get it over.

In the way of bush towns at that time, years could pass without anything memorable being in them. The towns could grow or decline, or do neither. There would be births, deaths and marriages, good times and bad. A man might get thrown by his horse and catch his foot in the stirrup, and get it out or not get it out, or be dragged until his head hit a rock.

The bank manager's name was Mitchell, when the twins were in their twenties. He had been city bred and educated and hadn't got over the fact that the Grey twins were readers. It was unusual to be a book reader, particularly in books that could be described as classics. There were many in bush towns then who didn't read the newspapers. He resolved to bring it up with Alec Grey, next time he had him in the office.

'There was a new parcel of books for you, Alec,' Mitchell said. 'I gave it to one of the boys.'

'Mathew,' Alec said.

Mitchell had put out the tots of whisky.

'Read a lot, do they?'

'They'd read the label on a bottle of hot sauce,' Alec said.

'Isn't that a bit unusual?' Mitchell asked.

'Not for the twins,' Old Alec said.

'Got it from you, did they?'

'From their mother.'

'I'm a bit of a reader myself.' Which wasn't altogether true.

'Nothing learned is a burden,' Old Alec said.

Mitchell had told his wife about the books the twins had read. There had been a difference of opinion as to who had encouraged them to read such unlikely things as Shakespeare and Byron. Old Alec had brought eggs and roses again that day. Before his wife had died and Alec Grey had altered, the manager would have never presumed to ask him about a family matter.

'It interested me,' Mitchell said, 'being a reader.'

'I can see that,' Old Alec said.

Mitchell had refilled the glasses from his hospitality whisky.

'I'm not sticking my nose in, am I?'

'Be that as it may,' Old Alec had said. 'You want to know about Mary.'

The manager had found that discomforting. With old Alec's eyes on him, not piercing as they could, more appearing to dream. He decided to drop the subject.

He said, 'How much do you expect to freight this year?'

'I don't mind talking about Mary,' Alec said. 'It can do her no harm. Soon enough it won't harm me. Good, bad or indifferent.'

36

Mitchell said afterwards that he never expected to hear what he heard. The change in old Alec had made him easier to deal with, but it had never been much more than that, him not having the same silence. There had been the first surprise of the eggs and roses and old Alec feeling his age. If his presence had diminished, it was nevertheless a presence, one not to take liberties with, apart from his importance to the bank.

'Today is the anniversay of Mary's death,' old Alec said, which greatly added to Mitchell's discomfort. It is hard to find something to say about the anniversary of a death, which can mean so much to one person and nothing to another.

He said, 'I'm sorry,' that catch-all for every purpose.

Alec Grey told Mitchell, who couldn't wait to tell it again, that his wife had come from Sussex. Her father had been a gamekeeper at Rutland Manor. The manager remembered that, old Alec naming the Manor. He had been the best gamekeeper in the country and a terror to poachers. The squire had liked and valued him. When Mary was fourteen the squire had taken her into the house. The mistress took to Mary, the way the squire had taken to her father. She had learned to read in the Manor, it must have fulfilled something in her and she was encouraged to use the library.

The squire closed the house and took his family to London on a visit. Mary had gone back to her parents' cottage during that time. She had gone to the marketing day in the village, walking with her father. Marketing days were boisterous affairs and her father had let Mary wander while he drank rough cider with the ploughmen, waggoners and thatchers. Mary would have frolicked with the boys and girls she had grown up knowing.

There had been others at the market on that day. They did the rounds of the markets, mostly on the lookout for gypsies and professionals who would steal the eye out of a needle. One of them caught Mary with something in her hands which should not have been there. Old Alec made no remark about the something, as to whether Mary was stealing it or taking a closer look. Mary was arrested. She appeared at the assizes.

There was nobody to help her; the squire and his wife were in London. Had they been in the Manor she would never have been committed to the assizes. Pretty little Mary was sentenced to transportation.

Mitchell said that he had needed another drink while old Alec was doing the telling. He said that it was harder than ever to meet those eyes, being taken back to the convict days, which everyone knew about without ever having seen a convict. Particularly with that great rock of a man telling it so gently, who had married the wife who had been transported, the Mary who had come down from the mountains with him and had been buried in the valley.

Mitchell said it had been hard for him, and that he couldn't help but wonder what Alec Grey might have seen when he first got to Sydney. Those years ago had been at the end of the transportations. If Mary had been a bonded woman, when Alec Grey met her, she must have been young when she had been transported. The manager had a daughter and he said that it gave him shivers when he thought about his daughter.

He knew that the hump-backed bridge had been built by convicts, which had little meaning to him other than knowing who built the bridge. But in the listening to Alec Grey, Mitchell said he could never think of the bridge again the way he had.

He had wanted to ask how and in what circumstances Alec had met Mary in Sydney. His imagination was on fire and he thought that he was looking at history, and hearing history out of that great rock of a man sitting across his desk. He said that the eggs and the roses, and old Alec having given up so much of his silence, could never impress him so much as learning about Mary Grey.

When Mitchell was being told about that long ago marketing day, it must have been at length. He said that Alec's voice changed, and his face changed, in the telling. Mitchell knew that he was sitting in the office of a bush bank, but he was also somewhere in England. Old Alec gave it such detail, his eyes more dreaming than ever, that he must have attended many such marketing days. He was speaking to be heard by Mitchell, but mostly he was talking to himself.

Since Mitchell was at a marketing day in England, before old Alec had been born, he asked him had he never thought of going home for a visit.

Old Alec said, 'A long spoon to sup with the devil.'

He had pointed to the basket he had put down on the desk.

'There are bantam eggs among the eggs. There isn't much in them. As small as they are there are other bantams in them. Bantam eggs have a way of their own. It's the shape and colour of them.'

It is odd that nobody got to the valley before Alec Grey. Ben Saunders had told everyone in the pub that he could remember back to when they were coming down the mountains with hardly a mile between them. They all had to cross the hump-backed bridge and they must have seen where the valley opened.

Gold seekers like Ben Saunders would never have stopped for the valley. They had no patience for a making, other than holes in the ground. Almost all of them buried their hopes in a thousand holes in the ground. Except for a few like Ben Saunders who had bottomed on old crooked seam.

The valley must have waited. Out of the stories, Alec Grey and the valley had waited on each other.

It would have been hard to miss a valley like that, with volcanic soil and a spring in it. A circling stand of cedar which was of the valley but not in it. It must have been hard to miss because the hump-backed bridge was narrow, and every wheeled and four-legged thing would have had to slow to cross it.

None of that explains why Alec Grey had to go on

breaking new ground. Why Tom Cosgrove saw the twins breaking new ground, soon after the death of their mother. Why they continued to do that, after the death of their father. Breaking new ground wasn't needed. They weren't struggling for a living. The valley was bulging and so was the account in the Warrawang Bank.

Why had old Alec never given up? He gave up some of his silence and made gifts of eggs and roses. He did not tell his sons to give up breaking new ground. He must have encouraged them when he was feeling his age. There is no evidence, out of the stories, that he ever advised them to stop. There was no rhyme or reason left to break new ground.

There was no living memory in the district to recall how Alec Grey had started. When the new settlers were pushing out to the plains and he had needed to scratch to keep going. Harvesting his first green corn and slaughtering his first mutton to trade with those who had to slow when they got to the convict bridge. Being grateful if a cart or a waggon had to be repaired, which he could lift by himself if it was a matter of repairing a wheel. Getting shillings for his efforts, or something the travellers carried which he could use. There was nobody left to remember that, except in stories as wild as wood pigeons. He was the miser now, the richest man thereabout, who had not spent to get a midwife when the twins had been born.

That valley was choking on things and enough was never enough. If old Alec had got too old to plough and axe and saw, the twins did it for him. They got more like their father each year, retreating into their own silence. When the Greys spent some of their money, did something with it that others could see, that would be the day. Envy in the town had turned into calumny. Why should one man have so much when so many were losing what they had? Worse than that, doing nothing with it except making more and more.

If Mary Grey had been a puzzle, it was certain that

nobody could guess at what Alec Grey might have been thinking. Mitchell had got something out of him at last, and had to tell about it. Mary had come in on the ball and chain. The story about her husband having been his own free man, could have been something that he had made up. He could have been anything in England. He could have been a murderer. In all those years he had never let anyone see more than the outside of himself.

If a man talks to another man, if only for ten minutes, he's going to give some idea of what he might be thinking. When old Alec's daughter had died he had admitted nothing to those who knew him then, other than the fact.

The stock and station agent who travelled about had been doing business with Alec for more than twenty years. So had the contractor whose men worked in the valley at pruning and harvesting. They both said much the same thing if they were asked. You could know Alec for twenty years and you'd know nothing about him. You could look into those pale grey eyes and be disturbed. You could get the impression that you were looking through them, all the way to the back of his head. And not get a glimmer of what might be behind the eyes. You could be sitting there with him, the great beard across his chest, dealing with him about pounds, shillings and pence, and you could wonder whether he was there or not.

It wasn't only the valley, it was that man in the valley. Afterwards, the twins, whom old Alec might have made out of himself by cellular division.

It was little wonder that stories got about. All the first makings in the valley Alec had done himself, with only his wife to help him. There were hundreds of makings being made on the other side of the mountains. There is only so much any man can make between sunrise and sunset. He can break his back at it, work by the moon or a hurricane lamp, but there are limits to what he can do. It had not been like that in the valley. The apple trees, the citrus, the crops that had to be sown, the house of cedar and granite. It is little wonder that it was said that Alec Grey must be a vital force.

None of that explains why he had never given up. Or why the two rocks off his rock never gave up. There was no rhyme or reason to it. That is why it had to be wondered who was doing the doing. The Greys could have been appendages on the valley. As was the spring that never stopped, the soil and the cedars.

Alec Grey had built the house on his own, although that was hard to believe. He hadn't built a hut to live in, after the tent, with a house many years away, a weatherboard house, but he built a house for the ages and many generations. A house like that might have been built after many years, out of a property founded and made secure, that had withstood floods and droughts. And so had the flocks on the property, increased enough and secure enough to warrant such a house.

He had wanted that house in the beginning, not waiting for many years, not waiting at all, mining and shaping the granite while the cedar seasoned and he and his wife lived in a tent. If there is a sin in pride and you're trying to beat the devil, or taking fortune by the forelock, Alec Grey had done it. There had to be downright disbelief that one man could do so much.

That got into the stories because there were men enough breaking their backs. They knew the limits of what one man could do. It had to get about that Alec Grey had not done it on his Pat Malone. It had to be flatly denied that he had done it without help.

It would have been natural to think and feel like that, because if you were driving yourself and had to hear about Alec Grey, it would not have been good practice for another man to have to measure up against him. If he did, it could make him feel like throwing in the sponge, or deciding that he must have something grievously wrong in him. He could not only break his back, he could break his nerve, being made out of such inferior material.

It would have been inevitable that Alec Grey would get into bush stories. There was the legend of a Big Alec, told by those who had no idea where it had come from. That Big Alec had jumped a river with a single furrow plough in each hand. He had eaten the snooker balls off the table in Bathurst, or Mudgee, or wherever it was being told, in mistake for hundreds and thousands. He picked his teeth with telephone poles and could blow a gale backwards.

Sometimes it was the Namoi River Big Alec had jumped, or the Condamine, sometimes he had eaten the snooker balls off the table in Moree, or Come-By-Chance. The story had been told long after the inspiration of it had been forgotten, or who had first told it and why.

Many with the land hunger in them had sailed for the colony when it became known that there was more land halfway down the world than anyone had seen yet or guessed at. Nobody owned it, this was land for the taking. The land hunger might always have been in those who took ship for Australia. If they could recite all their generations there might not have been an ancestor who had owned land. There were stories about immigrants who had taken up land bigger in area than the county they had been born and bred in.

If you got land like that, with everything God had put on it and in it, the land can put awe into a man. It could be hard for a man to tell himself he owned it. Nobody knew if God felt any sense of owning. When a man got into the land, the land got into the man. He would lie and cheat and connive and murder before he would give it up.

Nobody knew if Alec Grey thought like that because nobody ever knew what he thought. There were others out on the plains who owned a thousand times more land than he did. So much that they had to put outstations on it, had given them names like Briar Flat, Stony Creek and Dark Corner, Burr Downs and Kangaroo. They had to make a map of their properties so that they could keep it all in their minds.

Alec could keep the valley in his mind, keep it in his eye for that matter. That could have intensified it for him, intensified it for the twins. There is a difference between a woman seen at a distance, and a woman you can hold in your arms. Because it had been all the twins had ever known, the valley could have been like a cradle to them. With two graves in it and more to come, which were flesh of their flesh.

When what the twins had to do had been done, there was no necessity of love in it. It had already been postponed too long. The one thing the valley could not do was make another Grey. Only a woman could do that.

Why old Alec had not made it happen before he died is a different puzzle. It's a puzzle how he had been able to lay down and die without seeing a new human seeding in the valley. He would have known that the twins could not be fecund forever. It is possible that something had rotted in his mind. He might not have wanted to see another woman in the valley, not in his time, a woman who was no woman of his, usurping Mary's role and being alive in the valley the way his daughter never could be.

He might have seen to the end of it all. That could have been part of the silence which he only let down at the end. It is certain that if he had decided to get new seed, he would have done it. A word from their father would have been enough for the twins.

He could have had it talked out with the twins. If the other thing is the truth, that he knew what was to happen, it could make you give up religion or take religion up. He might have had a revelation and have seen all the way to the end. He might have seen a logic and a fate in it. His never ending breaking of ground could have been an act of despair. He could have imagined a judgment about something, which he had got out of his head or out of the Bible. There could have been a passion in him which he came to believe was a sin. To have lived for so long, with such silence in him, except at the end, suggests that he might have lived with something that had made him terribly wrong.

There had been a doctor in the town for years. He didn't ride horseback or drive a sulky; he drove a Willy's Overland Tourer. The twins didn't get the doctor to their father when he began to ail. Everybody knew about that because Tom Cosgrove had been saying so for months. Tom said it shook him up, to see old Alec, no more than a shadow of himself. The black beard, which had been grey for years, didn't seem to have enough flesh to hang to. The clothes old Alec wore didn't seem to have enough flesh to hang on. You couldn't believe that such a mountain of a man could become a shadow of himself.

The town was reminded of the Grey twins now, who wouldn't get the doctor for their father. They had always been different, drinking four beers in the Railway Arms and wouldn't hear bad language. Never taking a girl behind the church hall, where there was a depression with long grass and lantana in it. When you rolled a girl on the tiny flowers of lantana and the leaves that looked like mint, a bitter-sweet perfume came out of them.

Mathew had always been said to be more sociable than his twin. Young Alec had more of old Alec in him. Mathew told Tom, who had brought it up, that his father didn't see eye to eye with doctors. There were herbal remedies enough for anything that ailed you. All doctors knew was the knife. They couldn't wait to get a knife into you, out of any excuse they could invent. His father didn't see eye to eye with doctors.

Tom Cosgrove had argued the point; Mathew had put a hand on his shoulder. There was grey in his beard now. He had asked Tom how long he had known his father. He asked if he had ever known a man alive who could tell his father what to do. Mathew said that some men will take instruction. Some don't know who they are, or what they are, unless another man tells them.

Tom went back to the house on his next delivery.

'How's he doin'?' Tom asked Alec.

Alec had looked up the valley to the stand of cedar, which could be seen from the house because of its height, and the day was as clear as glass.

'He wants to die,' Alec said.

Tom told them in the Railway Arms that he had done his block.

'For the love of the Sainted Virgin.' Tom was a Catholic but horribly lapsed. 'He might be hurtin' down ter the pits of hell. You want me to stand here sittin' on me bum and not as much as a bloody doctor?'

'He knows what he's doing. He's told me and Mat what to do. He told us he's making ready to go. He won't go before that, or after that.'

Alec Grey would have died in the bed he had made, back in the beginning. His great calloused hands would have been on the patchwork quilt that his wife had sewn. His grey beard would have been over the cover, with his twin sons standing there, waiting. They would have waited in the half-light of the drawn curtains, with those startling eyes holding them tight and no words between them.

He had planted three thousand apple trees before he died, the acres of citrus and crop. The valley was a honey pot of growings and in the seasons there were twenty and thirty men working in the valley. There is a time to be born and a time to die, which Tom Cosgrove had heard old Alec say. There is a time for apple trees to grow old and fruitless, woody in the trunks and woody in the roots, with the sap withering in them. When apple trees get like that the good husbander cuts them down, and snags their roots out of the ground.

There was another thing Tom had to learn, and he didn't know whether it put him off his tucker or not.

Old Alec had carpentered his own coffin, as he had done two others. He had made it out of the cedar he had put by so long ago. He had taken the twins to the knoll with the two graves and the two markers on it. He had shown them the place reserved for himself, between his daughter's marker and the marker for his wife. He had told them what to chisel for him, which was simply his name and the two dates.

Below that there was to be one memorium.

HE CAME HERE.

When Tom was to see old Alec's marker, the dates of birth and death, he had done a sum in his head. In the town it was judged that Alec had to be over seventy. When Tom had done the sum it made him eighty-four. Even then nobody had known about Alec Grey.

There was another thing on the marker. The name chiselled was Alec Hannibal Grey. Nobody had ever heard about him having a Hannibal to him. On other papers and in the will, where a full name is required, there had been no mention of a Hannibal. When he heard about it in the bank Mitchell knew nothing about it.

He had said, 'There's a Hannibal, is there? Hannibal has crossed the Alps again. Hannibal and his elephants. Hannibal, the conqueror.'

What Mitchell had said got about. When Tom Cosgrove heard it, who had never heard of Hannibal or the Alps, he had asked a schoolteacher and had been told about Hannibal, the conqueror. Tom liked that; it suited his own idea. If Hannibal had crossed the Alps on elephants, which Tom did know about, without ever having seen an elephant, and had been a conqueror, it fitted the idea Tom had about Alec Grey.

It was many years before Alec Grey's full name came up again. Mitchell, the back manager who had known him then, had been replaced. He had been promoted to better things elsewhere and had done them. His replacement was Jim Kearns, who had been so upset and shaken when young Alec, who was still called that even when he was fifty, had come to town with the strange request which had been undertaken with such reluctance.

That comes later in the stories about the Greys.

Kearns and the solicitor had gone to the valley, and had been left alone in the main room. The family Bible was on the table, put on a square of velvet, hand-stitched on the edges. It had two clips to fasten the covers. It had pages of tissue when it was opened, tissues stained and fragile with age. After that there were heavy pages, with heart-shaped spaces on them. There were records of births in the Grey family, going back for generations, entered in the heart-shapes on the pages.

There was no entry there for an Alec Hannibal Grey.

Why had he been left out? The entries in a family Bible don't provide in its genealogy for such a neglect. Had Alec, Hannibal, been of the Grey family but not in it, the way the cedars were of the valley but not in it? Had he been born on the wrong side of the blanket, and his birth shunned in that genealogy?

The births of the daughter, Elizabeth, the births of Mathew and Alec, had been written into the Bible. There were other Hannibal Greys in the heart-shaped spaces. One of them could have been old Alec's father or grandfather.

If he had been a shunned illegitimate, remembering the time and place, he could have had a fever for land of his own making, if he had been disinherited of land in England. He could have had such a corroding resentment in him that it had turned his energies into that of two or three men. It could have had to do with the silence he wore.

The new bank manager was alert enough, and educated enough, to know that the names in a family Bible can also signify a class. There were Hannibals and Peregrines, a Mark Anthony, Elizabeths and Phillipas, and one Tudor Rose.

Names like that can signify acres, broad acres. The apple seeds that old Alec had brought with him from England could have been more than seeds to him. They could have been from a strain the English Greys had grown. If so, it was fitting that they should become Grey's Apples on the Sydney market, where Ben Saunders had seen that lettered and had taken a train to Warrawang.

Those seeds, to old Alec, could have been more than seeds with apple memories in them. They could have been seeds with memories in them for him, particularly if he had been disinherited and could have been in the main line.

His first plantings in the valley had been on the hedge-row principle. Later he had bench-grafted root pieces, the resulting plant to be budded over in the following summer. That knowledge would not have been the ordinary of an English carpenter. He could have learned it, being given work but not the name, somewhere his family had owned. His need of land and his bond to it could have been in the genes.

Whoever had reared Alec Grey, he must have been brought up on the Bible. If it had been his mother who had taken the illegitimate seed into her, or his father who had put the outlawed seed into someone else, there could have been a sickness for the sin.

It would not have been unusual in those times, in the circumstance of proud family, for the sinner to get as much of the Bible as possible into the fruit of the sin, so that it would not be repeated.

It is certain that the family Bible was the Bible in the main line. There were others to see it years afterwards, when it was being kept against a claim, because a family Bible going back so many years, into another country, can command attention.

If old Alec had been born a bastard and had to be disinherited for it, how did he get his hands on the Bible which would have been such a rent to those keeping the continuity?

A family Bible is kept by the head of the family, kept as a trust and responsibility and handed down. Unless the family was worn out and it doesn't matter any more. There was another thing that Jim Kearns saw that day. It was a faded, mildewed image inside the cover. He hadn't been able to make it out, but he thought it was a coat of arms.

49

If old Alec had been given the Bible, with his birth omitted, the person giving it must have been so moved as to be helpless. A family Bible in the main line is not lightly given, to be taken halfway down the world and never seen again. The intention might have been to give him the family that had been denied him. The family bound in the Bible, with no Alec Hannibal entered, in which he could keep his own line. None of those others to come in England could ever be entered in that Bible.

What's bred in the blood comes out in the bone, as old Alec had often been heard to say. He was talking about seeds then, and stock. He could have been thinking about something else.

The Grey Bible would have been as familiar to the twins as the backs of their hands. They must have noticed that their father wasn't entered into it. Would they have asked him about it? Would old Alec have told them?

They could have known that their father had shipped out of Liverpool, to find the place that had been ordained. That their mother had been a transported woman, and a bonded woman when their father met her. That old Alec had come from a family that bore a coat of arms, if that was the image inside the cover of the Bible. If that had been told to them when they had been judged old enough, and the reason why their father's birth was not in the family Bible, it would have been a load to carry. They were already different, being Greys of Grey's valley. If they had these other differences to carry inside them it is little wonder that they were remote.

It was also possible that the twins had been told nothing. Old Alec would have been too righteous to lie if he had been asked about the Bible. There would have been no reason for him to tell them about their mother. Certainly no reason for the twins to ever ask. Unless Alec had had his reasons and wanted them to know, for the story and the lesson in it, or for the simple sake of the truth.

It was unlikely enough that he had told Mitchell about

Mary. There had been no good reason for that. Unless he was becoming fuddled, being much older than anyone guessed. That day being the anniversary of Mary's death, she could have been much in his mind. His homeland and other marketing days could have been in his mind. He could have wanted another person to know, asking questions about the twins' book reading. He could have been caught in a weakness and was thinking aloud.

There was nothing that the twins ever said, unless to each other, to show that apart from the difference of being Greys, they had other differences inside them. After the death of their father, and both of them in middle age, they continued to work the valley. The work had become a disease, a disease of compulsion, an end and not a means. They could have been defying the English Greys to make more in one valley than they could have ever bequeathed. There had to be a reason, because there was no rhyme or reason in it.

The envy and the resentment in the town, the caustic and bitter edge that some tongues could manage in anything said about the Greys, did not ease with the years and the deaths in the valley. When Jim Kearns and the solicitor had seen the family Bible and had opened it out of curiosity, that had not been in the sequence of the stories. It was put there not to get too far from old Alec's second name being Hannibal. That it should have merited any remark describes the pressure the old man had always exerted on others. It describes his silence in all those years. The pressure that the valley exerted on others. The need in the district to learn something about old Alec that did not have to be invented.

The twins had been thirty-eight years of age when their father was buried on the knoll, with only Tom Cosgrove there. Young Alec had read from the Bible on that day. Nobody knows what the twins might have said to each other when they got back to the house. That house must have been evacuated to them, without the strong beat of their father's heart in it. They must have felt truly alone on

51

that night. They had no kith or kin known to them. Other than the names in the family Bible, out of England. Their father and mother were on the knoll, the little sister who was only a marker.

It is frightening to contemplate what the twins did before they died. The disease of putting more things in the valley, the breaking of new ground without rhyme or reason. It could be frightening to contemplate what they did not do. They could have committed a folly or a grand extravagance, which would have argued for their common humanity. They could have filled the valley with children, had meetings and picnics there. They might have sowed the one seed the valley had never known. The seed of joy and common weal, which can be a prayer in itself. They did the one and did not do the other. They were educated men and must have read because they wanted to. Out of their reading they must have learned about the human heart, circumstance and condition, the comic and the tragic. They did the one and not the other.

A new generation was growing up in the town and the district. They had no immediate interest in the Greys and the valley, as the older generation had done. But something of the stories must have reached down to them, because the children made up stories of their own.

There was a valley with two old men living in it. They set dingo traps around the entrance of the valley. The traps were to catch anyone trying to get in, who would be after the gold they kept in a chest. More gold than you could imagine. The brothers counted the gold at night.

One of the brothers was a hunchback. He would go to the entrance to the valley, picking his way through the dingo traps because he knew where they were. He would hide in the bushes on an old road. If you were silly enough, or brave enough, to go on that road, the hunchbacked brother would leap out of the bushes and catch you. Then he and his brother would torture you to death and eat you if they had a mind to eat you. If they just tortured you and didn't eat you, they would bury you on a knoll. There were hundreds of graves there, people they had caught that way. Every grave had a headstone with the name of the person on it. They had got the names out of torture.

Years ago there had been a father, and he was the most horrible of them all. He had the strength of a giant and was as big as a giant. The giant had a giant wife. Her teeth had been six inches long. She was almost as horrible as her husband. She tried to steal some of the gold one night and her husband ate her. There had been a daughter. The daughter had done something wrong and the giant and his wife had eaten her. They buried her bones where the others were, first licking them clean. The daughter the giants ate had been named Elizabeth.

The twins became distanced to the town after the death of old Alec. They were seldom seen in it, unless one of them had something to do in the bank. They had not been seen in the Railway Arms for many years. The town had got more prosperous and had other things to gossip about. A deposit of shale had been found not far away. The shale was to be mined for shale oil and work had started on that. There was new money in the town and new men and families with it. There was a pastry shop now, with big and little pastries in the window. The owner stood outside his shop in the evenings, wearing a white apron and smoking a cigar. It had been a ham and beef shop that had gone bankrupt.

A School of Arts had been built, with a library in it. The school that had been a bush school, one room and one teacher, was a proper school now. It had a shed where boys and girls could eat their lunches.

Grey's valley and the two Greys in it, became distanced out of the more important things that were happening. Only the old ones noticed it when Mathew drove to town in a new sulky. The one their father had maintained for so many years, which had been replaced in the wheels and the axle, finally despaired and had to be replaced altogether. This one had a buttoned leather seat, a holder for a whip and was in new paint with decorations on it. The older ones remarked, when they saw the sulky, about the cloud of moths that must have taken flight when the Greys had to open their purse.

The Greys and the valley might have become distanced, but legends and the makings of legends can renew themselves. It got about that a ghost could be seen at the old convict bridge. It wasn't a convict ghost, it was a ghost with a black beard. Sometimes it could be seen lifting a broken waggon with one hand. Sometimes it could be seen sitting on a wall of the bridge reading in a Bible.

Tom Cosgrove, who was getting on, swore that he had seen the ghost of Alec Grey at the convict bridge. Nobody paid attention to that. Tom had been suffering for years, what he called The Hathritus. He didn't do much more than sit on a chair on the warped and splintery boards of his verandah, and have the daughter who had not married fetch and carry for him. He also asked who would recognise the ghost of old Alec better than himself. Since, in his infirmity, Tom seldom volunteered to go anywhere, it wasn't likely that he had got himself out on the back road.

When the town began to spread, with the shale and other things, it had done so in the opposite direction to Grey's valley. That helped the valley to recede, not only in the mind. The twins were in their late forties now, and seldom seen in town, so much so that they and the valley were often forgotten. The valley was no longer the haunt it had been. The new road that had bypassed the convict bridge and the valley, meant that you wouldn't see it, or know about it, unless you went there on purpose.

The new sulky would have been something to notice, there were not many being driven then. There were motor cars in the town, later models than the Willy's Overland, which the first doctor had driven, when motor cars were not often seen. Nobody knew why the Grey twins had not got themselves a motor car. It must have had something to do with the flight of moths that would have to come out of their purse.

Would the Grey twins buy a motor car? Don't be silly. The Greys had not, and never would, give you the steam off their piss.

The one excitement in those routine years concerned a woman's magazine which had been newly published. Journalists and a photographer got off the train at Warrawang and asked for the valley. They were to make a magazine feature and lodged in the Railway Arms. That caused excitement enough, having magazine people in the town. It was hard to believe that the Grey twins would let strangers into the valley, not only let them in, but let them in to take photographs and write about it. Tom Cosgrove had to be asked, which meant going to his verandah. In any matter of fact or argument about Grey's valley, he was the authority. And would unfailingly put things to rights, when he had no more than a suspicion as to what was being talked about.

In this instance, he was unable to shed light on the magazine people. He admitted that he was flummoxed and had to shake his head and say that he never supposed to live to see the day. He had never expected to see the day the twins would let men with cameras swarm all over the valley. He got bad tempered about it.

The arrival of the magazine people got everybody talking. The town took it as a dignity for itself. Because the valley and those in it had receded, with no more than desultory talk for years, every story and memory became revived again. When the children heard their elders talking about it, that revived their horror stories. They had delicious giggles and shivers, if a magazine person was on the street, calling from a judged distance to look out for dingo traps. The older girls, whose interests were more gruesome, advised the strangers that they could be eaten when they got to the valley.

It became a four-day wonder. When the magazine people departed they took the wonder with them. Except for the impatience of waiting to see what would be in the magazine.

When the story and pictures appeared the copies of the magazine fell to pieces in days, through being passed around. The reason was that it had been the fiftieth year of Grey's Apples being marketed in Sydney. The story told how the apple seeds had been brought from England to Australia by the first Alec Grey. He had crossed the mountains with his wife and had settled in the valley. There was a bush ballad about him and stories of his ghost being seen near a convict bridge.

His twin sons were quiet men, proud of their heritage, but laconic about it. They had declined to be photographed. It was unfortunate that shots of the interior of the wonderful old house could not be got. The surviving Greys had said that the house was under repair.

There was a photograph of the marsh where the spring got up. Shots of the willows below the spring, which the first Alec Grey had planted. The orchard and the outbuildings with such captions as: Boxing Shed. One of the tool box Alec Grey had brought with him from England, showing its brassbound edges with the tools displayed beside it. One of an old waggon in a shed. The caption was: Early Apple Waggon. One of the stand of cedars, captioned that it was there that Alec Grey had got the cedar for his house. There were three pages of pictures and text.

It was afterwards learned from the contractor that he and the selling agent in Sydney had arranged the access with the twins. They had refused at first, until they had been persuaded by the contractor telling them that it would be a testament to their father.

There were those in town, after the magazine had been passed on, who got no satisfaction from it. It was a storm in a teacup, which hadn't touched the truth. There was nothing in the magazine about how old Alec Grey had trampled on others to get the valley, or how he had worked his wife to death. Nothing about his rich sons, who wouldn't buy a motor car. But would drive that sulky until it collapsed. And when it did they hoped it wouldn't happen until the horse had bolted and they going downhill over rocks.

Grey's valley became forgotten again. Everything was expanding. The district was expanding and other districts beyond it. Although there were still bad times for some, who shouldn't have got out of bed. In those years Grey's valley hardly rated a mention. The only thing to connect to the Greys was when old Tom Cosgrove died. Leaving nobody living to pronounce on the Greys and the valley, out of intimate knowledge and privileged information, even if he had to invent it. Old Tom had been sitting on his verandah, alive in the one minute, probably troubling his ageing daughter to get something for him, and dead in the next. Falling out of his chair as dead as mutton, without as much as a squeak. In a different way, a lot of Grey's valley died with old Tom.

There was another thing to happen, after the death of old Tom, that shook the town the way a dog shakes a bone. Because the Greys had been partly forgotten, interest was revived, the way it had been when the magazine people arrived in Warrawang. Having been partly forgotten, the revival of interest had a keener edge.

Jim Kearns was the manager in the bank at that time. The one who had gone to the valley with the solicitor, when they had looked in the Grey family Bible, which was put into the story for a reason, although it was out of sequence.

When he had taken over the bank he had been told about the Greys and shown the ledger of their account. Since the bank had been founded the Greys had banked in it. The interest on their account had almost become an embarrassment. In any dealings with clients, the Greys must be given priority. If that was remembered, it wouldn't be a difficult branch to run.

Jim Kearns was the manager on the day Alec drove to town in the sulky. He was dressed in collar and tie and wore a rusty blue jacket. If it wasn't in season, with dirtying work to do, the twins always dressed to drive into Warrawang.

When the teller saw Alec Grey enter the bank, he didn't have to be told, but hurried to advise the manager. The manager would straighten his tie and brush at his hair. They greeted each other and Alec took the customary chair.

'Glad to see you,' Kearns said, knowing not to offer a tot.

Young Alec, who was no longer young, sat with his folded hands on his knees, and they were humped and calloused the way his father's had been. His eyes were like his father's and he did not use preliminaries.

'Mathew and me are fifty today,' Alec said.

'Indeed,' Kearns answered, putting on a birthday face. 'A happy birthday to you both. And many happy returns.'

He said that he felt like a bug on a pin, the way he was being looked at.

'Mathew and me need a son.'

Kearns was city bred and not accustomed to directness. He and his wife drank sherry before dinner, in the thin glasses that had been a wedding present. He was certainly not accustomed to a statement like that, with no idea how to take it. In someone else it could have been a joke, but the Greys seldom joked. He also lacked his ordinary feeling of authority, because of the disproportionate size of the Grey account in the bank. He thought that he might not have heard Alec correctly.

He said, 'Beg your pardon, Alec.'

'Mathew and me are fifty today. We need a son to look to the valley when Mathew and me are gone.'

Kearns felt more than ever like a bug on a pin, with those unfaltering eyes on him, hard forged in the prism of fifty years in the valley. He had to know that he had heard correctly. He also had to find something to say.

'How can I help?' he said, having no idea himself and his wits going in all directions. Trying to hold to the fact that the Greys needed a son, and that Alec was sitting opposite and telling him that. He might have felt that he should have a son for them in one of his filing cabinets.

'In the city,' Alec said, 'there are women needing a husband. We want you to put a notice in the papers and get us a strong one. We want you to word it. She must be a respectable woman and she must be clean and healthy. We can offer her security and a good place to live.'

The state of confusion in the manager's mind must have been considerable. There would have been nothing he had learned in the profession of banking that would have helped. If he had felt the need to flatly reject such a wayward request, he would also have reminded himself that it was a Grey who had made it. Kearns smoked a pipe and probably lit it for support.

He asked, 'Have you thought this out, Alec?'

'It has been deliberated. Now is the time.'

'That being so,' the manager said, 'if you want me to word it. Having made up your minds and so on.'

'We'd be obliged.'

The manager was having further trouble, taking up a pencil.

'What will I put? That is, how will I put? What I mean is, something will have to said about the gentleman wanting to marry.'

'Landowner,' Alec said. 'Fifty years of age. Strong and in good health. Independent means.'

'Bachelor,' Kearns contributed.

'He'd have to be,' Alec said.

Kearns began making notes.

'I'd think the *Sydney Morning Herald*.'

He was desperate enough to try for a remark that would be both light and hearty.

'How do you think marriage will sit on you, Alec?'

'It's not for me,' Alec said. 'It's for Mathew. He's the younger one between us. Is that all?'

'I'll word something and get it away.'

Alec stood up.

59

'Have the answers addressed to the bank.'

'Tell Mathew a happy birthday,' Kearns said, showing Alec out.

In due course the matrimonial advertisement was published. Not in the *Sydney Morning Herald*, but in a publication that dealt in such notices. Kearns had passed the responsibility to head office, covered by a nervy, explanatory letter. The official at head office, responsible for country branches, examined the first replies, weeding out those deemed impossible and caused the notice to be published again. He interviewed applicants and made up his mind on one. It was hardly a bank matter, but exceptions had to be made for the Greys. He wrote a personal letter to Kearns.

That something concerning a woman and the valley became known in the town. Kearns had not breathed a word, other than to his wife, when he gave her an account of what had happened. It could have come from the station master. There were few unaccompanied strange women who got off the train in Warrawang. Particularly one who looked half scared to death and trembled so that it could be seen. She carried a cane bag of luggage in one hand, a purse in the other, and wore a small straw hat on her head. She perched on the platform seat like a bird that had been wounded, the station master said.

He had asked her, after some time, if she was waiting for someone. She told him yes, sitting on the hard seat with her cane bag on her knees, her purse on top of that and her hands holding to the purse. He wondered what Alec Grey was doing at the station when he saw him come out on the platform. The station master was at the end, watering the geraniums he was trying to grow. He went to refill his can and when he got back the woman and Alec Grey had gone.

The railway station was a half mile from Warrawang. The line had been built for other destinations and purposes. It had been down for a time before Warrawang had got a siding, let alone a station. Going from the valley to the station, the road skirted the town. Alec Grey was not seen driving the sulky with a strange woman on it.

He was seen in town next day, going to the bank. He was seen going to the Church of England. Confirmation classes were being held and the minister was at the church every day after school. Alec was seen coming out of the church, the minister with him, talking with him after he had got in the sulky.

Despite the reputation for being righteous, which went with all the Greys, neither the twins nor their father had ever attended a church service. It was wondered what Alec Grey had been doing at the church, still talking to the minister after he had got in the sulky.

Mick Grimes had a petrol bowser and a mechanic's shop behind it. He owned an old Buick, in which he drove travellers for Sydney to the station. A messenger from the bank had talked to Mick Grimes. The Buick was to be hired next day, to drive the minister, Kearns and the solicitor, to the valley. When Mick Grimes reported that, speculation became fevered. There was only one thing for it. Mathew must have died. Alec wasn't letting on about it, only to those he must. There would be a proper funeral to the knoll this time. This time, for the first time, it was going to be done right.

But hold hard. Why wasn't Bob Frew, who did tailoring and acted as the coroner, being collected in the Buick? The twins had got Bob Frew to backdate the death certificate when old Alec had died. There couldn't be a backdating this time, not with the minister and Kearns and the solicitor going out to be witnesses. It made no sense that Bob Frew wasn't going.

The woman who had got off the train and had been met by Alec Grey, because Chadwick, the station master, said they had both disappeared while he was filling his watering can, had to be a relative who had come for Mat's funeral. She wouldn't have come from Sydney for nothing. It had never occurred to anyone that the Greys might have a relative in Sydney. You didn't think about relatives when you thought about the Greys.

Having a relative could be another thing they had swept under the carpet. Old Tom Cosgrove had never made mention about a relative. If she was a relative, where did she fit in, and why had she never been seen in Warrawang before? If Mat Grey had turned up his toes, it could make you think. A big man like that, who hadn't seemed to change over the years, apart from going grey in the beard like his brother, with not more than a speckle of grey in his hair.

If it had to be one of the twins, better it should have been Alec. There had been more humour in Mathew. If Mat had been left alone there could have been socialising in him. He had always seemed to tag behind his brother. If Mat had been left alone as a youngster he could have been good company.

Mick Grimes' Buick was watched while it collected the bank manager and the solicitor and went to the church to collect the minister. You could see that it had to be a funeral, out of the way they had dressed up.

Alec Grey had it all now, everything in the valley and everything in the bank. What would he do, having it all? He wouldn't want to live there alone. It had been a long time since their father died. They had done for themselves in that long time; they had never needed a housekeeper or needed to get married. They had never fallen out over anything, the way some brothers can. They had stayed there minding their own business and adding to the valley.

Mick got back in his old Buick. He did not put his passengers off, because he had none. A funeral would take time and Mick wouldn't have been invited. It surprised nobody to see him pull in at the Railway Arms. Mick had time to kill and wouldn't have wanted to wait in the valley. He would have something to tell about it and others wanted to hear.

Mick looked a bit strange, ordering a beer, which others noticed by hindsight. They said, 'Mat fell off the Twig, did he?' They said, 'The first time there's been a proper funeral in the valley.' That was what Mick had supposed. He had been thinking about it on the way back to town. They asked him about the relative.

'Didn't see no relative,' Mick said. 'What I saw when I got to the house, when the Nobs were gettin' out, was Alec and Mat all dressed up. If Mat's a gonner, I never saw one like that.'

It was a thunderclap for the town to learn that Mat Grey had not died. That Mick Grimes had seen him as large as life and by no means a gonner. What was going on in the valley, the Nobs being driven there by Mick? Mick coming back to town because he had been told to collect his passengers much later on.

When Mick got in the Buick to make the return, the impatience to learn what was going on was painful to some. He was watched putting down the bank manager and the solicitor, driving the minister to the Church of England. Those in the bar watched the door for Mick to enter.

'What the blue blazes is happening?' he was asked as he came in.

'You wouldn't read about it,' he told them. 'I've got to wet my whistle.'

When he had put down the beer he told them again that they wouldn't read about it.

'The thing is, Mat got married.'

He looked at his stunned, disbelieving audience.

'No joking. Mat got married. He married that relative that got off the train.' Mick thought about that. 'What I mean is, he got married to whoever got off the train.'

When that thunderclap was heard all over town, there were as many who did not believe it as there were keeping an open mind. A Grey twin getting married, with nothing to connect it to, was an improbability too great for many minds to grasp. But Mick Grimes was certain about it, and he had driven the others to the valley.

When it had to be believed, because Kearns and the solicitor and the minister confirmed it, that Mat Grey had been married sure enough, speculation took up the woman. She had got off the Sydney train. That did not mean that she had come from Sydney. She could have come from somewhere on the way. Wherever she had come from, nobody had ever heard about Mat having a woman. He couldn't have been visiting her, because the station master would have known about it. You can only drive a sulky so far. So where had she come from and how had Mat got to meet her?

There was to be another thunderclap, a small one. Mick had remembered one of his passengers saying that the woman's name was Mary. He asked if old Alec's wife hadn't been a Mary. That was almost too much, a second Mary Grey coming to the valley. The first one had been worked to death. There could be a lesson in that, for the second Mary Grey. There was no way to work out how Mat Grey had got married. There had never been much that could be worked out about the Greys.

That was how the second Mary Grey had come to the valley. She had been Mary Gantling before that, married for ten years to a Gantling who had been killed in a quarry accident. She was small, like the first Mary, and proved to be an incompetent little thing. After the death of her husband, she had worked for six years as a cleaner in Sydney. She had a woman friend, with a sense of custody for her. Her friend had seen the advertisement the bank had put in the paper, and she had told Mary about it, and persuaded her about it.

It is hard to know, out of the stories, if the second Mary was one of nature's incompetents, or if she might have been simple minded. She might have been one of those plants who can only live in shelter. She might have been lost to any direction after her husband was killed, and her woman friend might have thought that answering the advertisement would be the best thing she could do. The official at head office, who had arranged the affair, told Kearns in his letter that Mary Gantling had a friend with her at both of his interviews.

To marry a landowner of independent means, who the bank would have vouched for, a healthy fifty-year-old man of good character, could have been more than Mary Gantling could hope for. Her friend could have known that she was too gentle and incompetent to exist on her own. She might have wearied of feeling a responsibility for Mary Gantling.

The official must have decided that she would be suitable for what had been required by the Warrawang branch. He would have provided her with expenses to get to Warrawang. Any expenses provided would have been a small thing for the bank, considered against the duty of servicing the Grey account. When Mat Grey's marriage had to be accepted as fact, never mind where his wife had come from or how he had met her, that gave rise to a question that had been forgotten for years. What would have happened to the valley if neither twin had married? They would both have to die some day. When that had to happen, if there were no children in the valley, what would have become of all the growing, the house and the out-buildings? Everything in the outbuildings and everything in the house? Not to mention the money in the bank. No wonder Mat had got married, to whoever it was. It was a wonder that their old man had not seen to it before he died.

When the marriage had been settled, in the minds of the town, it became the subject of ribald remarks. Both those twins, going back for years, and nobody had seen them give a girl more than the time of day. If one of the town girls, going back, had ever got a Grey up her, she wouldn't have kept it to herself. She'd have been more likely to shout it or get a sign painted.

What had the Greys done for a poke? Did they have a favourite ewe out there? Or had they done it with each other? Now old Mat had got himself married. He wouldn't know where to start. If they had been using a ewe, Mat must have got Alec to hold his wife by the head.

65

It was months before the townspeople got a sight of the second Mary Grey. She was in the sulky with Alec, not Mat, and waited while he went to the bank. She wore a straw hat and nodded and smiled at everyone. She was small, but a well-built woman, and what could be seen of her hair was black. Her features were neat and she didn't seem to have a line on her face.

There were women on the street shopping, making an opportunity to talk to Mat Grey's new wife. She spoke to them first, saying she had only been in the town once before. Not properly in it, only at the railway station. She thought that Warrawang was a pretty town. It had trees in it, she liked that. They should see the trees in the valley, where she had gone to live. There was every tree you could think of and the valley was filled with perfume. She told them that she had been married in the old house in the valley. The house belonged to her husband, or to her husband and his brother. She told them that in Sydney, where she had worked as a cleaner, there was nothing like the valley she had come to live in. The valley was like something out of a picture book. She hoped they would come and visit.

She was still chatting when Alec came out of the bank. She told them this was Alec, her brother-in-law. Alec smiled at the women and got into the sulky.

There was talk between the women on the street, after the sulky had left. And talk to their husbands when they got home. They had met the second Mary Grey, there was nothing stuck-up about her. She couldn't have been nicer, the way she chatted on. She said that she had been a cleaner in Sydney, which was a surprise. It was hard to imagine a Grey marrying a cleaner. Alec might not have liked that, if he had heard it. Mat's wife was a dear little thing, she had asked them to visit the valley. Everything could change now that Mat had married a sweet little woman like that. The valley, which had been as closed as a fist, from everything told about it, with no joy in it that anyone could remember,

66

had only needed a woman's touch, a woman like the one that Mat Grey had got.

Nothing changed in the valley, there were no further invitations, although some of the women hoped to see Mary Grey again. The dear little woman was not seen for months. When she came in with her husband she had not been so outgoing. You could see that she wanted to talk from the sulky, but she looked about her as though waiting on an alarm. The women made guesses about her age, because that was important. It was hard to guess about a face like that, with a skin that did not get wrinkles. A woman could be thirty and get wrinkles if she lived in the sun. Mary Grey could not have been in the sun very much, or there was something childish about her face. Whether that was the truth or not, she was many years younger than her husband.

Kearns was a good fellow, but city. He was on the right side of forty and serving his obligatory time in the bush. Both he and his wife were reluctant about it, but that was the system. By the time he was forty-five and had proved himself he could look forward to a good city posting.

Kearns was sitting in his office when he went pale on a realisation. He cursed his chief at head office, the man must have been mad. When he had described the successful applicant in a letter, he had said that she was a widow. She was acccustomed to marriage and would not be flighty about it. She had also been married for ten years and had not had a child. Good Lord! That had been the purpose of the exercise. Mary Grey could be barren. Kearns could see the Greys moving their account. He could see himself doomed to one-horse towns forever. It was winter and cold at the time, but he had needed to get out a handkerchief and wipe his forehead.

If Mary Grey appeared to be a simple person, so was Kearns and his chief. There had been nothing in the wording of the advertisement to suggest a sexual preference. There had been nothing about the applicant being

67

blonde or brunette, tall or short, or well-favoured. All that had been asked for was a female of marriageable age. Someone with a healthy womb, no matter what the womb had been put in. Or that was what the wording suggested to Kearns, when he thought about it and wiped his forehead. Mary Grey must be simple. Why would she have supposed that a healthy fifty-year-old, a landowner of independent means, would have wanted to marry her, if she knew herself to be barren?

She must be simple minded. At the ceremony she had had trouble answering yes in the right place. She had worn a tiny straw hat with a straw flower on it, and a chip of blue felt sewn into the centre of the flower, and had nodded the hat when she couldn't say yes. If she had known herself to be barren, and the responsibility for wording the matrimonial notice having been put on Kearns by Alec, he would bear the brunt of it if Mary Grey was a dud. Kearns thought further about it and cheered up. It wasn't a bank manager's job to be an expert on wombs. If nothing came out of the marriage, Mat could be a dud. If it went that way it wouldn't be his fault. If it went the other way, he could only benefit from it.

Mat had been married in the big room, under the tin-type of his mother. Near the cedar table and the cedar chairs and the willow chair that rocked. There had been fruit cake and port afterwards, and an offered bottle of whisky. Mat gave the impression that the wife, whom he had never set eyes on until two days ago, had pleased him. There was nothing reluctant in Mat, when he made his vows. He had appeared to be almost frivolous, which suggested earlier drinks in the house. There was nothing frivolous about Alec, although he had been more than pleasant.

You can suppose that Mary, having no idea of what she was going to when she sat on the station platform, looking like a wounded bird as the station master had told it, might have felt a lift in her heart when she saw the valley and the old house, smelled the tangy smell of apples and the waft from the roses in bloom. If she had been as terrified as she had appeared to be to Chadwick, sitting there with her cane bag of luggage and the purse she held on top of it, with no idea of what manner of man or place she was going to, only knowing that she was going there to marry, if she was accepted, to bed with the unknown fifty-year-old man and perhaps spend the rest of her life with him, it is to be hoped that her heart lifted when she saw the valley.

When Alec Grey had collected her from the railway station we don't know what he might have expected. There is nothing known about a possible exchange of photographs. Alec had collected the mail-order bride while his brother sat at home. Mat might have wanted Alec to get the first impression. Which they could then discuss after Mary had gone to bed in the room that had been prepared. Being married at fifty, with all that implied, would not have been easy for Mat. Out of everything known, the twins knew nothing of women, other than their mother and the sister they had never seen except under a granite marker.

It is hard to guess how Mat might have felt on his wedding night, going to bed in the room which his father and mother had slept in. When the ribald comments in town had said that Mat wouldn't know where to start, that could have been true for a fifty-year-old man who had never felt the need for it. Or if he had, for reasons of his own, or reasons he shared with his brother, had never made an overt gesture to do anything about it. They could have been too closed in, the valley closing them in.

If they carried in them the omission in the family Bible and the knowledge that their mother had been a transported woman, and carried that as a haunt, the way the valley was a haunt in itself, they might have taken up some of old Alec's communing and a different kind of silence.

The second Mary had been married and would have known what to do. If she had been simple it does not mean that she wouldn't have had passion in her. She might have been simple about it, with no concept of inhibitions. Simple women can be like that, simple and animal in their rutting.

If the twins had ever wanted it, that would have been easy. There were two whores in the town, not for money, but they would accept presents. One was married, the other was not, but they were whores out of a uterine hysteria, which could never get enough. If the twins had wanted no local involvement, they had money enough to go to Sydney for a visit and live any way that pleased them.

It could be, out of what was to happen, that there was no love in Mat's marriage. There could have been no love in that valley, so implacable with purpose. There could have been love in the second Mary, whose face was simple and childish and never got wrinkles in it. When her husband and his brother returned to the house at night, after she had served them at table and Alec had read from the Bible, she might have gone to a different room, after the time of consummation. Alec would have turned down the wick in the kerosine lamp and they might all have gone to bed in the dark. There might have been no night comfort for Mary, her leg on her husband's leg, his leg on hers, the warmth of each other and the sleeping breathing of each other, the unspoken community of sleeping breathing between husband and wife.

There had to be something wrong, desperately wrong, out of what had to happen. It wouldn't have been wrong to the twins. Despite their reading and more distanced understandings, they could have been appendages on themselves, as well as appendages on the valley.

When they considered, as they must have done, as Kearns at the bank had considered it, to wonder why a woman who had been married ten years and had never birthed a child, that realisation would have come too late, as it had come too late to Kearns. If they had considered, as Kearns had done, that Mary might be barren, that the womb they had got for themselves, because it would have had to be for themselves and not just for Mathew, the

70

second Mary Grey in the house might have been put away like bad seed. That could not change the fact that Mat had married for better or worse.

For three years after the marriage, at the usual times of pruning and harvesting, the crews came to the valley. There had been three thousand apple trees when old Alec died, now there were another five hundred. Although that count changed each season. Hundreds of old trees went bad each season, and had to be cut down and rooted out. In the pruning the dead wood had to be hauled away and burned. There was a place for the drying and burning, almost an acre of it. The granite poked through the earth there and it was a good place for burning. It was sheltered from the winds and there was little likelihood of sparks being carried to kindle a bushfire.

The crews said that Mary Grey was anxious to talk to them, if they were around the house. She would ask the men if they were married, and if they had children. The men said that you had to be careful, if your shirt was torn, because she would offer to mend it. If she invited them for a cup of tea, which she did, the men knew not to accept. The contractor had told them that if they accepted it would be as much as the job was worth. They also said that if she saw one of the twins coming that her hand would fly to her face and then she would fly inside.

In those three years and no sign of a child Kearns still felt uneasy if Mat went to the bank. Marriage meant a pregnancy to the townspeople, at least three or four, and more often than not it was a pregnancy that caused the marriage. After fifty years of waiting to get married old Mat couldn't get it up. If he did he wouldn't know what to do with it and it wouldn't have been any use asking his brother. Alec probably couldn't get it up and if he did it wouldn't have been any use asking Mat what to do with it.

It became taken for granted that Mary Grey was simple in the head. When she was in town waiting in the sulky she would talk to anyone about anything. She would chat away with the schoolgirls and had given one a lace hanky. The crews said that she would offer to mend things for them and ask them into the house. If she wasn't simple minded she was ratty. She continued to ask the women to visit her in the valley, although she had stopped doing that for a time. There wasn't a woman who would have visited if it had not been at the invitation of one of the twins.

When the joking about old Mat not being able to get it up had worn out, and because Mary would come into town with one twin and then the other, it was decided that they both must be humping her. The Greys had always kept things in the family. It was follow-the-leader in the valley. Two big men like that, with never a woman in the house before, apart from their mother, it was no wonder that Mary Grey was ratty. She might have been the full quid when she got off at the station, but three years of being humped by one twin and then the next, with nothing else to do out there and nobody else to talk to, would be enough to drive any woman ratty. She would have had to break them in, get it up for them and show them where to put it. She was well built if you looked closely and could be a bit of a goer, but with both the twins humping her she must be sorry she had ever started it.

The contractor had something to say about Mary. He said that you wouldn't know the house, or the big room which was the only room he had ever seen. He said that you could see her touch everywhere. He couldn't specify about it, apart from new cushions and the vases of flowers, but something had changed and you had to notice it. He said it was a pleasure to stay for a meal, not only for Mary's cooking, she had insisted he should call her Mary, but for other things such as the lamps she lit where the twins had only used one, and the starched check table cloth and the old silver which must have been in the family. And for the way she would buzz about serving, and talk about anything that came into her head.

He said the twins would smile as she chatted away but if

something displeased them, they would only have to give Mary a look. If that happened she would pale and silence and might not say anything for a long time.

That was the brighter side of the picture, because some of the crew who worked the valley had said that the Missus would sometimes come out for a walk. If the Grey men were in the orchard she would go to the other side. She would find something to sit on and try to talk to the men picking. She would try to help with the baskets and generally get in the way. She would stoop to look through the trees to see where the twins might be. If she saw one of them coming she would run back to the house. She had the sympathy of the crews, who liked the Missus and were sorry for her.

Mat had been married for almost four years when the jokes about his marriage changed. It was in the time of pruning, when many loads of lopped branches were taken to the drying and burning place. That shelf of shallow granite wasn't far from the house. There was much coming and going from there with over three thousand trees to prune. The Missus had been seen doing things outside the house, feeding the fowls, getting things from the store shed. One of the men had gone to the tool shed which was the closest outbuilding to the house. It was hard to see in the tool shed if you had come out of the sun. He said it had given him a start to see the Missus there, sitting on a box.

He had asked what she was doing. She told him that she had done something bad and was being punished for it. He couldn't believe that, but it was odd to find her there sitting in the gloom. She didn't seem like someone being punished, she seemed as perky as ever. She had been wearing an apron over her dress and she put her hands on the apron.

'See what I've got?' she asked.

The apron had a pocket but the man couldn't see anything in it. He wanted to get out of the tool shed.

'What is it?'

'What is it, you silly man, can't you see?'

He got the tools he was after and started to leave. He didn't want to be found in the gloom of the tool shed with the Missus.

'Are you married?' Mary asked.

He told her he was married.

'Any children?'

He told her two and tried to get past because she was between him and the door.

'Then you must know what this is. It's a baby.'

The man said she had rubbed her stomach the way you can do after a good meal.

'All in there,' she said. 'What do you think of that?'

If that wasn't believed at first it had to be afterwards. Mary Grey didn't carry high as some women do. She carried low where the first months have to be seen. The men who came to work the citrus after the pruning, said there was no doubt about it, Mat's wife was carrying. Boy or girl there was going to be an heir for the valley. When that got known in town there were still a few jokes. There were those in the Railway Arms who wanted to know which of the twins would be father to the child. What with both of them humping her, they would have to toss for it. One thing was sure, whichever twin the child favoured wouldn't make a difference. If it came out looking like the one, it would have to look like the other.

As Mary advanced in pregnancy she was not seen in town. With the apples and the citrus needing culling, because the age of the trees was getting out of hand, there were men in the valley for months at a time. They said that when you saw the twins with the Missus, not one but both, they had their eyes on her like hands. Not eyes on her face, eyes on her belly. If the Missus was about they would watch every move she made. And always on the swell of her belly. If she tried to do anything that might have been an exertion, and one or the other saw her at it, she would be stopped by a look, or a hand on her arm. They said that if she didn't

74

seem to be well, which she didn't, it would have been hard to be well with those four eyes of the Grey men never leaving her belly. Always on her belly as though they might have been four hands.

A group of men had come down to sharpen axes on the big old carborundum wheel, one to turn and whet with water while the other put a blade to the stone. Mary Grey was returning from the fowl yard carrying a basket of eggs. She must have tripped on something and fell on the eggs. They said that they heard a roar. It was both of the Grey men, going to the house, who had seen her trip. They said that while they stood there poised, startled by that roar, they saw her get up and back away. The broken eggs were dripping on her and the basket. She held the basket to her while she backed away. She was crying and her face was twisted and a high note came out of her.

She cried out, 'No! It's mine not yours. I've got it inside me. I'm the mother, it's mine. It isn't yours, do you hear? I'm the mother. Leave me alone. It's mine, not yours.'

They said that after that they had trouble sharpening their axes.

As more months passed, the regular workmen in the valley began to worry about the Missus. Her feckless chatting had gone, she looked pinched in the face and on the shoulders. If she came on a man unexpectedly she would start back, as though at a threat. When she moved around the fowl yard or the outbuildings, she would scurry to get it over. There were small marsupials in the orchard that would dart out for a crust that had been left, quivering at the risk of it. The men thought the Missus had got like that. You'd have thought that the twins would have been happy. There had been no human seed in the valley for over fifty years. You'd have thought that they would be pleased and proud with an heir to be born at last. If they were they didn't show it. There were seldom two twins up the valley at one time. They seemed to take it in turn to have one of them near the house.

The contractor noticed a change in the two Greys. There was always paper work in the seasons, tallies for each man's work, which the twins had always insisted in going over in detail, more paper work at harvesting when everything had to be accounted for. That would be done in the house, on the cedar table. Alec always took charge, delegating to his brother. The twins had always been righteous about the paper work, not only checking a man's tally, if they thought he was over-claiming, but also checking in his interest if they thought a mistake had been made.

If the contractor was engaged with them, and Mary passed through the room, they would stop and watch her until she had left. They would watch her after she had closed a door behind her, as though they might have been able to see through the door. If a reference had to be made to Mary, in the hearing of others, it was never to Mary. From Alec and her husband the reference would always be to Mrs Grey. When they were doing paper work at the table, if Mary had not been seen, one twin might ask the other if he had seen Mrs Grey.

Alec had the head for figures. The contractor said he could keep a season's accounting in his head, and if there was a difference of opinion between them, and the contractor had to look up his records, he said eight times out of ten Alec would be right. Now he made mistakes over the cedar table or appeared to lose interest.

Once again it appeared to others that there was no joy in the valley, with what you would have thought now to be an occasion for joy. The Grey men had become more remote, Alec more than his brother, and he had a touchiness about him which the workers had to watch. The men said that if something went wrong, and the Missus dropped the child before its time, they wouldn't care to be in the valley when that happened.

Mary Grey must have been driven to a desperation to do what she did. She must have been terrified by her own fragility. No pregnant woman can guarantee that nothing could ever go wrong in the foetus she carried. The crushing weight of responsibility, the weight of those eyes that never left her belly, and all the things that might have been said, which only she and twins could know, must have been too much to bear. She had been married to a Gantling for ten years and had not borne a child. She might have impregnated in that time and lost it. This pregnancy could have been more precious to Mary than the purpose of the twins. She might not have wanted it to have a purpose, other than the purpose of being loved. You don't have to have the curiosity of a face that did not wrinkle, and give the impression of incompetency, and chatter away to anyone who would listen, not to have deep and private feelings.

She would have been in her seventh month when she did what she tried to do. Both twins must have been up the valley, to give her the chance. She must have learned how to harness a horse to a sulky. She packed the cane suitcase, put on the straw hat she had arrived wearing and had worn when she was married. The one with the chip of felt sewn into the straw flower, to give the straw petals somewhere to come from. She knew the road and drove it to the railway station. She could not have known if there was a train to Sydney that day.

Chadwick was out on his station when she arrived. He saw her come in, bent sideways by the weight of her bag and the weight of her belly, bulging and making it difficult to move. She sat on the same bench where he had seen her when she got off the Sydney train four years ago; there was only one bench. She tried to get the cane bag up to sit on her knees. She couldn't do that because of her belly, she had no lap to put it on.

Chadwick didn't know what was happening and he went outside to see if one of the twins was there. There was only the sulky. She had not tied the horse, the reins had been left on the harness. The horse stood with his head dropped. Chadwick got the reins and tied them to the old hitching rail. He went to the ticket office and put on the kettle to

77

boil. The way she looked she could do with a strong cup of tea. He made the tea and took two mugs to the platform.

He asked Mary where she was going. To Sydney, she said. He did not tell her that there was no train that day. He knew that something was wrong and one of the twins would come in. There was nothing he could do, except provide tea and company. She asked him if he had children. He told her four, two boys and two girls. She asked about their ages and appeared to perk up.

She asked Chadwick if his wife could sew. Mary had made the dress she was wearing. He could see that she was having a baby. She hoped that it would be a girl, so that she could sew pretty things for her. Chadwick had biscuits in a tin and went to get them. Mary said they were her favourite biscuits, milk arrowroot. The best way to eat them was to dip them in the tea. She told Chadwick that she had never had a baby before. She used to pray for one. It was strange having a baby, you could feel it. You could feel it right up next to your heart. She asked Chadwick if he could feel it, and took his hand to put on her belly. She told him the baby was all in there. The baby was inside her and when it kicked you could feel it.

Chadwick had asked her why she was going to Sydney. Didn't she think that she would be better at home? He said it wasn't a good idea to travel, if you were going to have a baby. Repairs were being done to the line and it could be rough on the rails. He suggested that it would be a better idea to go home. He would see her into the sulky. He knew that she must have run away and wondered when one of the twins would get there.

'Home?' Mary had asked. 'I had a home, but that was a long time ago. I was married then, but we never had a baby. Not like this one, you can feel with your hand.'

'Home to the valley,' Chadwick said. 'They must be worried about you.'

'My husband?' she asked.

'Yes. Mat must be worried.'

78

'Alec?' she asked.

'Alec too,' Chadwick said.

'I can't do that,' Mary said. 'I'm going to see Daisy, Daisy's my friend. I don't know what happened to Daisy. I wouldn't be here if it hadn't been for Daisy.'

Chadwick asked if she'd like more tea. She said yes, and asked for a milk arrowroot biscuit. When he was getting it, Chadwick went outside and looked up the valley road. There was no sign of Mat or Alec. If there had been a train for Sydney he wondered how he could have stopped her getting on it.

'When is the train?' Mary asked, when he got back with the tea and biscuit.

He told her there was no Sydney train. There would be one tomorrow.

'We can't wait that long,' Mary said. 'My baby and I can't wait. The baby can't bear it. It's making the baby sick.'

She had cried a little then, Chadwick had seen the tears come out, although there was no sound of crying.

'I don't know what to do,' she said.

'Never mind,' Chadwick had said, and tried to pat her on the knee.

He was sitting with her on the seat, when Alec Grey came out on the platform. He first stood in the arched entrance to the platform, Chadwick could see the sweat on his face and the way his face was disordered. He stood there, taking deep breaths, before he went to the bench. Chadwick said that when Mary Grey saw him, she looked like a rabbit being hypnotised by a snake.

Alec nodded to Chadwick, put his hand on Mary's shoulder.

He said, 'It's time to go home, Mrs Grey.'

Mary Grey had got a hold on her bag. Alec had taken it from her.

'It's time to go home,' Alec said again.

'Nice meeting you,' Mary had said to Chadwick, as Alec helped her up the platform.

Alec had ridden in. His horse was lathered when Chadwick went out to see Mary Grey being helped into the sulky and the saddle horse tied behind. He said afterwards, being enough disturbed to try for what he had felt, that he had never seen a face so empty as the face on Mary Grey.

Chadwick had to tell his wife about it. She had to tell the neighbours. Mary Grey had tried to run away, at the end of her time. Why would a dear little thing like that try to run away to Sydney when she was too heavy with child to walk straight? What had the twins been doing to make her want to run away? They were no better than their father had been, there were stories about old Alec.

The men who worked in the valley had been saying for months that something must be going on. When they were getting an heir to keep the valley alive, what had they been doing to Mat's wife? She might be a bit simple, but the contractor had said that she kept a good house. He had spoken about seeing her touch when he had stayed for a meal. How she would get all the lamps going and put out a starched cloth and old silver. And what a good cook she was, with three or four vegetables, if it was a roast. And raisin pudding and custard after, or semolina pudding, or treacle roll, and if it wasn't custard it would be cream.

It hadn't been Mat who had gone to the railway to get her. It had been Alec. The men had been telling dreadful stories, but some of it could have been true. You would think, if you had a wife who had run away, that it would be the husband who would get her. He was the married one, not Alec who had gone to get her. The men were always thinking up something to say about the Greys. Things you didn't want to hear unless you had to. They were a dirty mouthed lot, the men. You had to wonder, hearing that Mary Grey had tried to run away, if there might not have been something in it.

She had tried to run away, Alec had got her and taken her home. The workmen had been saying that by the look of her she was about to drop any minute. There was something about their father not getting a midwife when the twins were born. That was an old story, it might have come from Tom Cosgrove. Maggie Miller was the midwife. Maggie hadn't heard from the twins. They hadn't asked Maggie to be ready if one of them came to town. They might have made an arrangement with Doctor Miskell. It wouldn't take him long to get out there in his car, if Mat's wife went into labour and one of them came to get him.

It had been harvest time in the valley when Mary Grey had her child. There were men everywhere, men around the house doing the boxing, trucks leaving the boxing shed to go to the railway, men stencilling the boxes, cart loads of apples being brought from the valley in their baskets. Although the contractor was motorised the carts were still used. The valley, which had an echo, was filled with noise. The sound of a baby might have been going on for days before it was noted.

The cry of a baby can be heard over other sounds. There is something in it that pricks the ear. The men had thought they might have heard a baby crying. They couldn't be sure and asked each other about it. There wasn't a man who would have asked one of the twins. When there was no more doubt, one of them having gone to the house and put his ear to the wall, every man in the valley stopped what he was doing. The Missus had delivered her baby. It had been a baby crying all the time.

Maggie Miller hadn't been seen. Doctor Miskell hadn't been out in his car. The twins must have done it themselves. Some of the men, who were fathers, had something to say about that. Others, more kindly, told them to hold hard, the Missus might have been caught short. There might not have been time to get Maggie Miller or the doctor. Whatever had been the strength of it, there was a baby sure enough. That was why Mat and Alec hadn't been seen much for days. Good on them. They had something now to keep the valley going. Those who had been thinking that one day it would be up for grabs, had another think coming. If the Missus has been caught short, and the twins had to deliver the baby, they would rather it had been them than the men doing the talking. When Mat and Alec got over it, there might be a celebration.

It was still Mat and Alec more than it was Mat.

With the birth of a child established, there was another thought to have. What was it crying in the house, was it a girl or a boy? The twins would want it to be a boy, but a girl was better than nothing. There hadn't been a child in the valley for over fifty years. If it was a girl, and took after its mum, it would be pretty. You could see that the Missus had been a good looker. She wasn't all that bad now.

The twins had delivered Mary the way their father had delivered them. It had not been a sentiment or a principle. It was out of the closed-in life they had lived which had been like that when their parents were alive, and out of their communing with the valley. They had lived their lives as closed as a fist. They had no reference or model as to how to be any different. When they had got the womb that was needed, that had been their affair. The birth was their affair, it was not to be shared with midwife or doctor.

They must have known that there could be risks in a birth. They must have taken that risk. They might have believed that a risk would be God's will, not to be changed by midwife or doctor. They had been obsessed by the child before it was born, there might have been no room for the others.

For a week the men heard the new-born cries, the pale thin bleatings that can sound like a new-born lamb. They felt different as they did their work because there was a new life in the valley. The presence of new birth can focus the mind, like the presence of a new death. Those who had invented reasons to dislike the Greys, who never had a good word for them, had to be pleased that an heir had been born.

Mat was seen out of the house, talking to the truck driver.

The truck was taking a load to the railway. Most of the men were camped on the drying and burning area. There was a long shed there, partitioned into rooms, with a verandah to it. Outside, there was a granite fireplace, with the base of an iron bed fixed into the granite. On the close-knit meshing, a sheep butchered into cuts could be grilled on the bed. Some of the men had brought tents.

When the truck returned from Warrawang it stopped in the living area. The last daylight was going and the men were walking back from the orchard. Mat came out with an apple basket and put it on the truck. He told the driver that there were fruit cakes in the basket, he and Alec would be over later. There was an eighteen-gallon keg on the truck, got from the Railway Arms by the driver. When the men walked back the keg had been tapped.

They became boisterous drinking the beer and eating the cake, taking looks at the house. The twins hadn't said a word about the baby, but they were doing the right thing. They quietened and nudged each other when they saw Alec and Mat coming from the house. Mat was carrying a basket, with two handles on it. He put the basket on the tray of the truck.

'Who made this bloody good cake?' one of the workers asked.

'That was Mat,' Alec said. 'He's good with an oven.'

'How about a toast?'

They said that Mat's face gave nothing away.

'A toast for what?'

They felt discomforted and shuffled about.

'What do you mean?' Alec asked.

That made it worse than ever. The twins might have got the keg and the cakes to wind up the harvesting season.

'Isn't this a bit of a celebration?'

They said that Alec seemed to be thinking about it. He asked his brother what he had in the basket he had put on the truck. Mat said he didn't remember, he'd have to take a look. He got the basket off the truck tray.

'Don't know what this is,' he said. 'You blokes had better take a look.'

The child whose crying had been heard was in the basket, asleep on a pillow. The men crowded to see it and were told that it was a boy. They lined up, punching each other on the shoulder, declaring that it was a little ripper, and telling each other to look at that, and telling Mat good on him. They asked what was he going to be called.

'Alec Hannibal,' Alec said. 'After his grandfather.'

It was some time before someone thought to ask about the Missus.

'She's well,' Mat said.

'A bit tired,' Alec said.

They wanted to ask how the twins had managed the birth, because it was the last thing that any of them would have wanted in their lives. You couldn't ask a thing like that, which didn't stop them thinking about it. They had been surprised enough that the baby had been brought out of the house in a basket. They all felt good about it being a boy, they could imagine how the twins felt. When the twins had taken the basket back and the keg was getting low, the men became maudlin, because the twins had done the right thing at last. They said that you could say what you liked about the Greys being bastards, wouldn't give you the steam off their piss, and the stories they had heard about their old man stepping on everyone to get the valley, but there were no two ways about it, they had done the right thing today.

When the eighteen-gallon keg was emptying, arguments had started about the stories that had been heard. It didn't matter a tinker's damn if the old man had come out on the ball and chain. He had made the valley and the twins were keeping it up. If they had to be different, that was their business. If they'd both been humping the Missus, that was their business. As for the stories about their father's ghost having been seen at the convict bridge, there was nothing wrong about that because some of them had seen it themselves. It was a shame old Tom Cosgrove was dead. He'd

84

have liked to be in the valley today. The little Missus had done the right thing, having a boy. It was going to be Alec Hannibal. What kind of name was Hannibal? They had never heard tell of a name like that, they wouldn't give it to a dog.

The news that a boy child had been born, that the twins had delivered it, that it was to be called Alec Hannibal, went through the town. Jim Kearns sent for a bottle of port, to be kept in his desk drawer and not to be opened until one of the twins came in. He had long forgotten his apprehension that Mary Grey might be barren.

That the twins had delivered the child caused offence. The women said that might have been well enough in the old days, when a man out on a selection had no other choice, but not in these days with a midwife and a doctor in the town. There was something dirty about a man delivering his own child, let alone the father and his brother. If Mat's wife had been caught short, that didn't stop it being dirty. Nobody knew what went on out there.

Other things got back in the next months. The boy had a good crop of hair but he never seemed to stop crying. If you were around the house for most of the day, he wouldn't stop crying. What had been seen of him looked all right, but there were no two ways about him being scrawny. If you saw him without a sheet on, one of them had, he wasn't much better than a skinned rabbit. His legs and arms weren't much better than pipe stems. It made him look out of proportion, when you saw that against the size of his head. If you didn't know better he could have been born at six months.

The women told each other that Mary Grey must have dried up. If what the men said was true, that baby could be starving. Nobody had got more than a glimpse of the mother. She had not looked well before the birth, and looked no better now. She would have things on her mind, having tried to run away. It was criminal that Doctor Miskell hadn't been asked to go out. If Mary Grey had dried up, the child should be on the bottle. What would the twins know about making a bottle for the baby? They might give it milk straight from the cow, everybody knew these days that straight cow's milk could make a baby sick. There were those who said that straight milk had things in it that could kill a baby.

They wouldn't be surprised if that baby died, the way the twins were going at it. Dingo Parker's young 'un had been born before its time, and would be about the same age. Dingo's young 'un wasn't scrawny. It already looked big enough to get up and run.

After two months Alec Grey drove into town. He went to the bank and the solicitor's office, who did two days in Warrawang and three days away. He went to the Church of England and called on Mick Grimes. Two days after that Mick got the old Buick out. There was to be a christening in the valley.

That was like those old men, having a christening at home. They couldn't have it in the church like ordinary people, with a font in it for christenings and an organ. Oh dear, no. They would have to get the baby christened in the valley, with only a few of the Nobs. What kind of name was Hannibal, anyway?

It wasn't Mat who was having the christening at home, it was they, the twins. They, had delivered the child. They, should know about straight milk. They, had put on the beer keg. Mary's necessary part in the birth was almost forgotten. They, had got an heir for the valley. The men, who had seen her in glimpses, said that she looked a bit crook and that there had been no chance to congratulate the Missus. She had been different before that, when she seemed to scurry about and had looked frightened if she saw another face. You might have thought that she'd have come out when the beer and the fruit cake was on. When the twins had done the surprising thing of bringing the baby out of the house, in a basket for everyone to look at. You'd have thought she'd be proud and want to be seen. That she would have wanted to come out with the basket.

The baby would have been four or five months old before the next thing got back. There were often men in the valley now, working at odd jobs. In their time the twins had added to everything. They had added to the apples and the citrus. The flock of sheep was getting out of hand and they had to be crutched and sheared. There had been additions to the roses and they were getting out of hand. When lambs were born they had to be ear-marked, and tailed, the male lambs castrated. When the sheep were sheared it was done in a pen. Old Alec Grey had not gone in for wool, but for mutton.

The twins had been letting the sheep multiply, instead of selling them off. Something had to be done about crutching, if they got fly strike in their dags. Something had to be done when they were rolling in wool. The valley was getting out of hand, but that did not stop the twins adding to it. The itinerants would roll a cigarette and talk about it, when they became familiar with the place. They would ask each other what did the bosses think they were doing? Did they want to jam the valley until it busted wide open?

There was a felling and grubbing of old trees going on in the orchard. The twins had got three local men to do it. They had known the men as youngsters, when they had been youngsters themselves, visiting the Railway Arms. They were more easy with them than they were with strangers. The men, who might have made abusing remarks about them, had long ago worn out their prejudices. You couldn't afford to be like that, not knowing when you might be in need of work in the valley. In any case the Greys were the Greys, that was all there was to it. They had known the Missus over the years, she remembered their names. She had always asked for a name, when she was chatting with someone, and had a memory for names and faces.

The christening had gone off well enough, but Alec Hannibal had not stopped crying. Both Mat and Alec had held the child. Mary had been nervous and distracted. She had not held her baby for the christening. When it was over she had not stopped for port and fruit cake. She had snatched at the baby and had taken it from the room. Mat had gone to the kitchen to make a bottle and had taken it to the child. After a time the crying had stopped.

Mick Grimes said that when he had gone to get the Nobs in the Buick, he had heard them saying on the drive that the mother had not held the child.

What got back from the men culling the orchard, was that if Mat or Alec went up the valley they took the baby with them. They had a basket for it and an umbrella to put up over the basket. They would put the basket in the shade and then put up the umbrella. They would use their feet to heap a bed of old leaves and put the basket on it. If the baby cried, one of them would go back and squat at the basket and rock it.

They would say to the men, 'Growing, isn't he?' The men couldn't see that he was growing. They said that they didn't like the idea of the twins taking the baby up the valley. The baby should have been with its mother. What if an old branch was to fall, when the basket was under a tree? What if a funnel-web spider got into the basket? In any case they didn't like working close to a crying baby. There was a time and a place for everything.

It seemed an unnatural thing to do, day after day. If the Missus was crook and couldn't look after the baby, it was bloody high time one of the twins got Doctor Miskell out. The Missus must be more than crook to be unable to look after her baby. All she'd have to do would be to feed and change it. Anyone could do that, you don't feed a baby all the time. You feed it once, you don't feed it again for hours. The Missus must be bedridden, or something. If she was, why hadn't Miskell been out? There'd been no bloody sign of him, or they would have seen the car.

If it was a matter of feeding the baby, one of the twins could have done it when he went back to eat. They had always carried lunch up the valley, now they went back to the house to eat. They could have fed the baby when they went back. They didn't have to bloody lump it with them, wherever they went. You'd think that if they took their eyes off the baby, it might disappear. It would be enough to make anything cry, being lumped about like that.

The chance that Mary Grey might be bedridden, because there had to be a reason for the twins carrying the baby about, had to be soon dismissed. The local men saw her in the fowl yard and hanging out washing. They only saw her from a distance, but she was having no trouble getting about. You had to scratch your head about it, ask yourself what were the Greys up to now. The Missus often used to wave, if she saw men and was outside doing something. That had been before she got pregnant. She had always moved as quick as a bird. Now, from what you could see, she was dragging herself. If she could go to the fowl yard and hang out washing, she could look after her own baby.

It brought a chill over the men who worked the valley that year, when it was realised that there was no physical reason why Mary Grey could not care for her baby. Whether she might have been well or not, the twins took the baby from her. They had to keep it close, where they could put their eyes on it, the way they had put their eyes on it before it was born, the way they had kept those eyes on Mary's belly.

It made some of the men sick when that was realised. Each day that baby was taken from its mother. She had not agreed to it, because something was heard that made the men feel worse. Two of them had gone to sharpen axes on the old carborundum stone. The wheel of the stone was grooved in the middle through many years of use; it was close to the entry of the house, where the first Alec Grey had put it.

One of the men stopped and asked the other if he had heard anything. They both listened, one man's hand on the turning handle and the other with a blade to the stone.

89

They heard the cry from inside the house. One said it could have curdled the milk in your tea. It was Mary Grey crying out from somewhere inside.

She was crying out, 'My baby! My baby! They won't let me have my baby.'

One of them must have been more sensitive than the other, or he might have had a child of that age.

He said, 'That does it,' and threw the axe to the ground. He got his things from the hut on the burning area and walked into town. He told them in the Railway Arms that the Greys ought to be shot. He would like to do it himself, with a few other things before the shooting.

When what had been said became known, it wasn't gossip about the valley this time. It was more uninhibited tongues that were allowed to wag. It came out in a few words, with shakings of the head. Everything else, over the years, had been something you could take in. The Greys had done it this time.

It was the season of growth in the valley. The season of bird migrations to the marsh where the spring got up. The leaves on the apple trees were vibrant green and apples were being budded. The visiting birds were all colours. There were galahs in the cedars and mountain rosellas picking for food. The goldfinches, diamond sparrows and red-heads, were in the hedges of privet. There were tits and silver-eyes in the briars and on the blackberry bushes. The wild duck who had far to go, were dropping down for a rest.

The valley nevertheless, had become dark to others, who had a heart. The Greys had taken the baby from its mother. There was no more to say about them. You wouldn't want to know about a thing like that. The Greys had done it this time. There were others with deeper thoughts, which they might have found hard to voice. Were the Greys in that valley, or was the valley in them? Did they have the child inside them, the way they were inside the valley? The valley had never been shared with others. From what was told, the first Mary Grey had to lay down and die. From what was

90

told, there had never been a communicated joy in the valley. Now the second Mary Grey, who had always been a dear little woman, even if you had only heard about her, the second Mary had had her child taken away from her by the twins.

The truth of it lowered voices. This wasn't like the stories of old Alec, or the twins when they were young. This was something you didn't have to hear from someone else, something going back years ago. This was now, there was no argument about it. One of the men had heard Mary Grey cry out that her baby had been taken away. There was nothing you could do about it, except feel about it. You couldn't understand about the valley and the people who had lived in it. Mat had got married to a woman who had got off the Sydney train. He had got a son by her. He and the brother had taken the baby from the mother.

That was known and remembered when the crews came in for the pruning. They tried to show their disapproval in their voices and eyes, if they had anything to say to Mat or Alec. Some of them spoke out, letting the twins hear it, asking each other if that baby shouldn't be with its mother. The twins ignored it. Every suspension of the child's breath seemed to be a suspension of their own. If it did not catch the next breath, all the Greys might die. If it did not, the valley could die.

Mary Grey was bereft of her baby from morning to night. Bereft of its baby smell and the cuddling and feeding of it, the washing and the powdering. Unless she had the baby to herself when the twins went back to eat. If she did, that might have made it the harder when they went up the valley again. When the child was toddling they continued to take it with them. When it was walking they began to leave it at home. When the child stayed in the house, one of the twins stayed with it.

The Missus could sometimes be seen, doting on her baby. She had got grey in the hair, which she had always worn pulled back in a bun. The face that had not wrinkled had

91

lines in it now, lines as fine as a spider's web, around her eyes and mouth. All her chatting had departed. If one of the men spoke to the Missus she would often look blank, and appeared to have trouble making a response.

When the child was five or six, the blonde hair was down to its shoulders. It could have been a girl, if you didn't know better. The twins sometimes had the child riding on their shoulders, one leg each side of the neck, the child's hands on their heads for balance. It called its father Papa, and it called its uncle Papa. The child was growing tall for its age, but it remained noticeably scrawny. It had baby words now and would speak them, if one of the men had something to say while the child was riding on Mat's or Alec's shoulders.

When Mat took the boy to town, to be fitted for shoes and other clothing, driving the sulky with the child sitting between his legs, everyone wanted to see young Alec. He was shy and would bury his head on his father. Mary Grey had not been seen in the town since she had tried to run away. That had not been forgotten, the way the child having been taken from her had not been forgotten. You would have expected Mary to be in the sulky and doing the shopping for her child. He didn't favour his father, he looked much more like his mother. He had a keen little face, blue eyes like his mother's, the same thick and shining hair. If he had not been properly fed as a baby, that showed up. He was thin, much too thin.

Mary Grey began to speak to the men, if she got the chance. She would ask, 'Have you seen Alec Hannibal? Isn't he beautiful?'

There wasn't much more that could be got from her, other than the question. When she was answered she didn't seem to remember and would ask again, 'Have you seen Alec Hannibal? Isn't he beautiful?' Sometimes she would add, 'He takes after me, you know. There's none of the twins in him.' If she was more than usually agitated she would come close enough to whisper.

'You don't think so, do you? You don't think he might

92

have the twins in him? Don't you think he takes after me?'

It worried the men to see Mary like that. So agitated and asking her questions. It had been said that she might be simple minded, but this was something else. The men didn't gossip about it, but they talked between themselves. The Missus had their sympathy, knowing that the baby had been taken away when it was only months old. Some of them said that if it hadn't been for needing the work, the Greys could stick their valley up them.

Young Alec got to be seven and eight and he had not been put to school. The school had a new building now, a big weatherboard room. That was the infants' school and it was thought that the twins would have taken advantage of it. The children had felt mats to sit on, while the teacher played nursery rhymes on a piano and taught them the words. And a blackboard to teach the alphabet. The Greys could have bought a car to get young Alec to school.

If they were not putting the boy to school, they must be teaching him at home. It was said that the twins had never been to school. Whoever had taught them must have been good at sums. If they didn't know anything else, they knew how many pence there were to a pound. How many farthings to a penny. They wouldn't give you the steam off their piss, but they would know the weight of the steam. They'd know how much an ounce the steam would be worth.

The twins were over sixty and a lot had happened in the town. It had grown with the shale oil, grown as a marketing centre. There had been many births and deaths over the years, many tragedies and joys. The valley had become more important than ever, and was often mentioned now in newspapers and magazines. Which raised little interest, unlike the excitement when the first magazine people had come to Warrawang. The increase of traffic on the highway, which had years ago by-passed the valley and what had been the only road when it had first come down from the mountains, made the back road further recede by being so

93

busy. Grey's valley and those in it receded. Tom Cosgrove was dead and gone. There were no more folk with long memories to talk about the valley. And less and less interest if anyone had done so.

It was seldom that a man on horseback was seen in the town. There were still sulkies being used, but not many. Doctor Miskell's surgery was in a solid house, originally on an old property which had failed and been forgotten before the town became a town. There were small hills in the town and Miskell's house and surgery was on one of them. It had become known as Doctor's Hill, and had a steep rise. Boys had to be punished for bowling motor tyres down the hill, which would get up speed and go leaping down the main street causing trouble.

The main street began at the foot of Doctor's Hill. A road there came in from the left. If the road was followed it led to the valley, taking a fork a mile out. The street and the shops were busy at midday, and busier a half hour later, when the school came out for lunch. There were children on the street when Mat Grey came in at a gallop. His horse almost fell when he wrenched it to turn up Doctor's Hill, the school children there scattering. The rider was seen from the main street, flogging the horse up the hill. It had to slow on the steep rise and sparks came from its shoes as the horse slipped on the blue metal that had been dug into the surface. Everyone on the street was looking up to Doctor's Hill. Some of them recognised the rider to be Mat Grey.

They made themselves into groups. The Greys never came in on horseback, certainly not at the gallop. Something had happened in the valley. It must be bad for Mat to have gone galloping at the hill, to get to Doctor Miskell. There was nothing to do but wait, before it could be learned about. They waited on the street, looking up to the hill and talking about it. They could see from there, when Miskell came out with his black bag, both he and Mat running for the Doctor's car. Miskell came fast down the

94

hill and skidded the car when he turned it into the road out of town. Those on the street eddied about, telling each other that whatever had happened it must be bad. If something had happened to the boy, the Greys would go out of their minds.

When those who had been in the surgery had walked down the hill to the main street, they were met by those walking towards them. They wanted to know what had happened, what had been said, and what did they hear Mat Grey say? He had rushed through the waiting room to Doctor Miskell's surgery. A woman had had a child inside, having its tonsils looked at. Mat Grey had rushed right into the surgery. They heard him say something about somebody dying. They didn't know if it was the boy or not. He had said something about a cut on the throat, or a cut on the wrist, or on both. Miskell had slammed the door shut, before he ran out with his bag. They didn't know what would happen to the horse. It was standing there, all in a lather, where Mat Grey had got off. One of them thought he had heard something said about a scythe.

Something bad had happened, that was for sure, they had heard Mat Grey shouting that someone was dying. They had heard him say that Alec was trying to stop the blood. Someone must have cut themselves on something. If Alec had been trying to stop the blood, it couldn't be him who had cut himself. It had to be the boy, or his mother. There was nothing to do but talk about it, and make speculations.

Next day the facts of the matter were learned from Miskell's receptionist. It hadn't been the boy, it had been Mary Grey. She had fallen on a scythe in the tool shed. Doctor Miskell had been out there all night, but he hadn't been able to save her. Later that day, Bob Frew, the tailor and coroner, was seen being picked up by Mick Grimes in his old Buick.

Most of them had seen a scythe, with its long, reaping blade and long bent handle, with another jut of handle on it to help the other hand, when crop or grass was being scythed. They had seen the long, curved blade on a scythe, it could take the leg off a man if he got in the way when someone was using a scythe. If Mary Grey had fallen on a blade like that, and Mat Grey had said something about the throat, the blade of a scythe, if it had been kept sharp, could take a head off. Something had been said about a wrist. If you fell and got your wrist on a scythe, it could take your hand off.

Mary Grey had fallen on a scythe and Miskell hadn't been able to save her. She was dead out there, in one of the rooms. It must be hard on the boy, never mind old Mat and Alec. All he had known was his mother and father and uncle. He hadn't been put to school to know other boys. He must be eight or nine by now, and you could feel things hard at that age. The twins could be bastards, they had proved that when they had taken the boy away from its mother, but you wouldn't wish a thing like that on your worst enemy.

When there had been time enough for the horror to soak in, there were shrewder opinions. Look, just put it all together. She had tried to run away, when she was almost ready to drop the boy. Old Alec had to go to the railway and get her. She had been heard years ago, crying out to herself that the twins had taken her baby.

She had hardly been seen since the boy was born, and when she was she would ask her ratty questions. She might have fallen on the scythe. And she might have not. She might have used that scythe. Who had ever known what went on out there? The twins could have driven her mad. Mary Grey might have done herself in. What would she have been doing in the tool shed, with the scythe against the wall, falling on it so that she got cut in the throat and wrists? There was no doubt about the throat, Bob Frew had seen it. He was shaken up when he got back from being the coroner. You only had to talk to Mrs Frew to know how

96

shaken up he had been.

All the stories out of the past rose up, out of the horror for Mary Grey. The first Grey had been a murderer out of England. He had come in on the ball and chain. There had been someone in the valley before him, he had disappeared. That was how the first Grey had got the valley. His wife had died mysteriously. She could have done herself in. There had always been secrets out there. That was why Mat and Alec had always kept themselves apart. You could count on the fingers of one hand anyone who had been known to overnight in the valley. There was a story about the first Grey having set the entrance with dingo traps. You wouldn't do that if there was nothing to hide. If there was a nigger in the woodpile this time, nobody would ever know.

Bob Frew's verdict was death by accident, which had to go on the death certificate. It was better for the boy to grow up not knowing that his mother had suicided. Nobody blamed Bob Frew, he had done what was best.

There was another burial in the valley. The Nobs attended. Kearns, the bank manager, the solicitor who was doing his days in town, the Church of England minister. The same Nobs who had gone out there when the boy was christened.

There was no port and fruit cake after the ceremony. The boy had been crying. A coffin had been got from town and was already in the hole which the twins had dug. They didn't cover it while others were there. They nodded their thanks and took the boy back to the house. He walked between them, with one arm around each. Kearns had his own car now and he drove the others back. That made four graves on the knoll near the house.

The twins were seldom seen in town after that. If one of them had to come in, still driving the sulky, they might as well have been somewhere else for all the recognition anyone got. They did not bring the boy with them, he was only seen in the valley. It was known that Kearns sometimes drove out on business. The boy was growing up. He knew almost nothing of other boys and girls. The men working the valley sometimes took their children with them, to help their father for a few days and for the holiday of it, before they were taken home at the weekend. These were the only boys and girls that young Grey had ever met.

Vic Forbes sold the Railway Arms and moved to Sydney. He sold the hotel to a younger man who had recently married. Both he and his wife had come from Sydney; she had been a school teacher. She was bright and energetic and immediately took an interest in the school. She took an interest in the valley, when she first heard stories about it, and a particular interest in the boy who had so shockingly lost his mother. She announced that she was outraged to learn that the boy had never been to school. There were laws about a child attending school.

Warrawang might not be a metropolis, but she hoped that it was civilised. Everyone had to go to school, the state wasn't bringing up a generation of illiterates. If the Greys were too shiftless to drive the boy to school, they could have arranged for him to board in town during the week. If they were as rich as everyone said, the aristocrats of the district, they could have sent him to a boarding school in Sydney. She had got herself on the school board and made the outrage of a ten-year-old boy never having been to school into a project for herself. After all, things had changed. If the Grey brothers had never been to school, that must have been fifty years ago. It wasn't only in the boy's interest, it was a matter of law. She spoke to the headmaster about it and she spoke to the Parents' and Citizens' Association.

When the school inspector arrived on a visit, he was brought into it. He had never heard of the Greys or the valley, and the ten-year-old who had been kept from school, and had to ask questions. The new wife, who had taught in a good Sydney school, taught secondary classes, paraded her knowledge at him. The school inspector did not travel

98

by car, he travelled by train to inspect other schools out on the plains. She arranged, at her expense, for Mick Grimes to drive the inspector to the valley in the Buick that wasn't getting any younger.

When the inspector returned he spoke to the headmaster and took the next train to Bathurst. The headmaster spoke to the former teacher. The inspector said that he had arrived at the house and stated his business. He had been invited inside and had asked about the boy. The boy had been out on his pony. He had talked to the twins and had been offered tea and fruit cake. He had said that he couldn't get over two big men like that, with the same beards and the same eyes and so alike from what you could see outside the beards, that he couldn't tell which from which. He said you could smell apples inside the house and that there was a patina on the old cedar. He had been surprised at how well-spoken they were. There was an old tin-type on the wall, he wouldn't guess how old, a woman in the tin-type and there was something about her face. He said everything in the house had an other-world feel about it.

He had told the Greys about the law, that a child had to be got to school, or good cause had to be shown why not. He said that the one who had spoken as the father didn't answer. He had looked to his brother. The brother asked who had sent the inspector to the valley and he told them it had been through the Parents' and Citizens' Association.

The brother said, 'The boy knows his three R's. He won't know more than that. He has no use for a school.'

Alec had asked his brother to get the boy. The inspector said that when he lifted his mug, the size of his hand put it from sight.

Alec had said, 'You know boys. That's your job. You'd know there are boys and boys. There some who can figure, but can't do their letters. Some have this coloured hair, and that. Some can carry a tune, where others can't.'

The inspector had wondered what was coming next, the

brother's eyes on him while they waited on the father to come back with the boy.

'Our boy's different. He wouldn't have any use for a school. Or a school have use for him.'

The inspector had been surprised to notice a book case. It was a big one and full of books. He had tried to read the titles on the backs and the few he could surprised him. The brother noticed that and said that he and his twin had been taught to read by their mother. There were other books in another room. The inspector felt bound to say that might have been all right then; he was there about the boy. Times had changed. It was law to put a boy to school.

The brother continued, not moving his eyes from the inspector.

'One boy will see one thing. Another boy will see another. Our boy mightn't see what another boy sees. Our boy sees what he sees.'

The inspector said that when the father came back, he had the boy with him.

'This is Alec,' his father said.

'Alec Hannibal,' his brother said.

He said that the boy had shrunk back on his father's legs. He had a hat in his hand and was twisting it.

His father said, 'We have a visitor.'

The boy had struggled to get it out. It twisted his face, the way he was twisting his hat.

He said, looking up to his father, 'How do you do?'

The inspector had tried to talk to the boy, which was hard, he said, the boy in such difficulty and the men with their eyes on him. He had asked him to do a simple addition, and would he tell him, in his own words, what he had been doing that morning? He had asked him to spell cat, and mat. He saw that the boy was handicapped, it wasn't a matter of school. He saw that it wouldn't advance him to be got to the Warrawang school. The inspector had been dealing with boys for years. He knew a handicapped boy when he saw one, and knew that nothing could be done for him in a state school.

The boy had asked could he go out, both the men had nodded.

'Is that all?' the uncle had asked.

The inspector said that when he was taken outside, the boy had been talking to the car driver. Not close-up talking, talking from a distance. He couldn't hear what he was saying. He was either talking or making noises. He seemed to be well dressed and well fed, the inspector said in his report. He might have lung trouble later on. He was pale in colour and pinched in the chest. His shoulders were bony and narrow. He wasn't without intelligence. He was handi-capped and would never fully develop.

In the town, where there had been such curiosity about the boy, even before he had been born, when Mary Grey had run away, the weathercock of gossip changed. It hadn't been criminal of the Greys to keep the boy from school. The boy was retarded. His mother had been a bit simple. You'd have to be more than simple to do what she had done. The Greys had been doing as best they could, having a boy like that. When you got down to it, and never mind the money, there hadn't been much luck in the valley. When you got down to it, thought about it and remem-bered, it might be better to be in your own shoes than in the shoes the Greys wore.

The Greys wore those shoes another four years, before the next thing to happen happened. It was after the fall of leaves in the orchard. That began by the leaves being rasping and dry on each other. The stems that kept them on the branch got dry and began to wither. When they were ready to fall, nothing might happen if the valley was windless. When a wind whooshed down from the cedars the leaves would fall in clouds. The orchard would be full of leaves falling. If the wind had a spiral in it they wouldn't fall first, but go up off the branches, whirling and floating and blowing about until the wind let them down.

When the branches were becoming empty of leaves, as

naked as a man stripped of clothing, the leaf fall became feet deep under the trees. Every variety of small rodent and marsupial, spiders and centipedes and caterpillars, made home in the mulching leaves. Black snakes, brown snakes and tiger snakes fed well on the others living in the leaves. This was a good time for kookaburras. It was a good time for hawks, who would glide over the orchard looking down with their gimlet eyes. And dive with their talons stretched before them, to sink into something small. Everything was eating something else in the orchard.

The kookaburras conducted a different operation. They did not glide high, spying. They came in and sat on the bare branches, their interest in snakes.

They would sit in the bare branches, looking absent-minded, quizzing their heads from side to side. Then they would plump down and snap a snake behind the head. They would stay there with the snake in their beak, looking absent-minded again. Then fly up to a branch and hold the snake. From their beaks the rest of the snake would be writhing and thrashing. The kookaburras would perch on the branch, looking uninterested in their catch, fluffing chest and wing feathers, raising one foot after the other, coming out of the leg feathers like feet out of trousers.

When the big kingfishers had established that any audience must have appreciated the brilliance of the catch, they would gobble a few more inches of snake through the yellow clappers of beak, with a hook at the end of the top beak, then dash the head of the snake on the branch. And keep doing that with thumps that could be heard from a distance. Not in rapid succession, but after many a delay in which it would seem that the bird had forgotten what it had in its beak, and hadn't killed yet.

In that time Mathew Grey was doing something in the orchard, walking his ankle boots through the leaves, which were dry on the top and mulching below. He would have been keeping his eye out, because he had been brought up knowing the dangers in the orchard at that time. The tiger

102

snakes could have been breeding, with the fierce instinct to protect, the time when a tiger snake will attack. Mat said that he had felt the weight of the snake at the first impact. It sank its fangs above the boot, a fraction lower and it would have missed the flesh. The hyperdermic needle of the fangs pumped from the venom sack. Mat told his brother that there must have been two of them, he had felt another impact through his trousers on the calf of the leg.

He had got out of the leaves onto hard ground and had cut at the two purple dots above his ankle with the folding knife he wore in a pouch on his belt. The snake must have got its fangs tangled in that strike, because he had needed to knock it off with his hand. When the blood came he had squeezed at the wound to get the venom out, then he had pulled up his trouser leg to get at the second strike, to lance it with the knife and squeeze at the blood. Mat was thick in the muscle and bone and he was over sixty then. He couldn't get his mouth to the wounds to suck at the venom.

There was condes crystals in the house, the bush antidote for snake bite, but it was a long way to the house. The poison was at him before he got back, feeling the nausea and the dizziness and beginning a kind of fever.

Alec had squeezed and sucked at the wounds and rubbed in the condes crystals. He had used a leather strap for a tourniquet, pulling it tight above the knee. Mat had used his boot laces, they had wedged into the flesh. Alec must have despaired when Mat told him it had been tiger snakes, that one had to be knocked off his trousers, and how high in the valley he had been. The blood circulates faster in running and walking. It has to circulate and pass through the heart and Mat's blood had been poisoned.

Alec had harnessed the grey gelding into the sulky, a new grey now, out of the breed his father had started. The boy would have been crying and helping, he had been taught about snakes. Mat would have needed support to get to the sulky, the world would have been sick and spinning to him.

For the second time in five years there had to be a dash

for Doctor Miskell. Alec flogged the horse up Doctor's Hill. There were patients waiting and Alec rushed through them, startling the receptionist and bringing Miskell out of his chair. He and Alec got Mat inside while the girl got rid of the others. The town had a small hospital. When Miskell had done what he could do Mat was taken out between the doctor and his brother and driven to the hospital. Tiger snake venom can be deadly, more at some times of year than others. It was the worst time, if the tigers had been breeding.

Mat had been miles up the valley, it had taken him time to cauterise his wounds, more time to walk and run back. More time for Alec to work on him, harness the sulky and drive ten miles. It had been hours before Mat was got to the doctor. There was no anti-venom stocked then. Mat was over sixty. He was delirious before his heart gave out.

The boy might have been handicapped, but he knew what had happened to his father. He was tall and skinny and pinched in the chest, but there can be a lot of tears in a fourteen-year-old boy.

It was late at night when Mick Grimes was got to drive out to the valley. Mat had been put in pyjamas and had a blanket around him. The boy sat in the front seat, his head in his hands, making sobs. Alec was in the back seat, holding the blanket that had his twin in it. Miskell had offered to drive him back, offered all that he could, saying over and over to Alec that he was sorry. He would have felt bad saying it, because he had said it to Mat and Alec when he couldn't save Mary Grey.

When they got to the house, Alec went in and lit the lamps. He came back for the boy and took him inside. He asked Mick to help him. There was a sofa in the main room and they put the weight in the blanket on it. The boy must have gone to his room.

Mick asked old Alec if he wanted him to stay. He didn't mind how long he stayed, could he make him a cup of tea? Alec got two glasses and a bottle of port, the only drink ever seen in the house, back to their father's time. He sat with his head hunched into his beard and moved a chair so that he could sit with one hand on the blanket.

He said, 'A time to be born, and a time to die.'

He wasn't saying it for Mick Grimes, he was saying it for himself.

He said, 'Even though I walk in the valley of the shadow of death, I will fear no evil.'

Mick Grimes didn't know where the words had come from, but he said they had a ring about them that he seemed to remember. He seemed to remember having heard those words, somewhere or other.

Alec said, 'One old man and a boy in the house. Only one old man, now. One old man and a boy, to be left in Grey's valley.'

Mick had listened for the boy, but he could not hear him. He said he saw the blanket move and it frightened the life out of him. He saw it stretch, where the legs would have been. It had seemed to hump for an instant, where the knees might have been. Then it stretched out and flattened. When he was telling it, afterwards, with time to think about it, he had heard that dead bodies could move before they stiffened.

Old Alec had his hands to his face, Mick said nothing and watched. He drank the port because he had never had a dead body in the car before. Then he saw something coming out between those lumped and calloused fingers. He knew then that old Alec was crying. Mick knew that there was nothing he could do, old Alec crying like that. He had got out of the house as silently as he could. When he started the car he had winced at the noise it made.

Mick said he had never felt so bad in his life, driving away in the dark. Knowing that in that house there was one old man and a boy. And the other old man in the blanket. He couldn't describe the room to his wife, when she asked about it. He didn't know if it was big or small, or what it might have had in it. Other than one old man crying in the room, and the boy probably crying in another, and the old man in the blanket, who had been attacked by tiger snakes and would never cry.

There was still horror in the locals about the death of Mary Grey. Now, this had happened. All in five years. And the boy, the only young Grey, was not developed in his mind. One thing was repeated, it had nothing to do with a flight of moths from a purse. If the twins had bought a motor car and learned how to drive it, Mat might have been got to Miskell in time to save him. If Mat hadn't needed to gallop from the valley on a horse, when what had happened to Mary Grey happened, if he had been able to get to Miskell in short order, she might not have died.

If the twins had hardly been seen in town, after the death of Mary Grey, old Alec became a recluse after the death of his brother. The seasons of others continued, out of habit it seemed. The habit of the contractor, the habit of the working crews, the habit of the station master. The habit of the bank manager, who had to drive out now to get his business done. Mick Grimes delivered supplies, the way Tom Cosgrove had done. He drove out in the Buick and put the supplies in the box. He would read the note that would be left there, about what next to bring.

The boy would be up the valley early and late when the crews came in. He would ride his pony bare-back and go down between the trees in the orchard. He would bring a lunch and tell the men what was in it, and how he had cut it himself. He would tell them to look out for snakes, because snakes could kill you. And show them the snake-proof boots that he wore. He didn't seem all that retarded, to some of the men. If he got a stutter up and made sounds with no words in them, that was only excitement, having had no one to talk to other than old Alec. He didn't look anything like his father, or his uncle. The twins had always been craggy in the nose. You couldn't know much about the rest of the face, because of the beards, just the nose and the eyes and the cheeks, the hair that was kept cut short.

Old Alec had taken to cutting the boy's hair. A few years back it had been as long as a girl's.

Old Alec didn't move far from the house any more. He was no longer everywhere at once, being stern at anything he disapproved and writing on a paper with a pencil. He didn't tell the men who were still using the horse drays, that the wheels needed greasing, or that the tailgate had lost a chain. He didn't tell the truck drivers not to drive fast over ruts, which would bruise the apples. That apples were gentle things, and had to be treated gently. He could be seen around the house pruning the roses or feeding the fowls, chopping wood for the stove, or repairing the door on an outshed or sitting on a form mending harness. He had little to say to anyone.

When the boy was up the valley on his pony, he would ride back to the house every few hours and could be seen with his uncle.

The men told each other that old Alec had dropped his bundle, after Mat had been bitten by the tigers. Both twins had dropped their bundles after the Missus had cut herself, but they had got over it, or had come to terms with it. Old Alec showed no sign of coming to terms about Mat. Old Alec had dropped his bundle.

Mat's funeral had been on the third day after Alec had taken his brother's body home in the blanket. Kearns, the minister and Bob Frew had attended. Once again no other townsperson had been invited. Alec must have laid the body out and made the preparations. It was wondered if the boy had helped prepare his father's body for the grave. In that time Alec Grey had carpentered a coffin. It was not a bought one this time. He built it in cedar, the same old cedar that was on the knoll in three other coffins. The boy had looked stupefied, Bob Frew said. Being backward, he might not have had much idea of death. He had an Adam's apple in his long, thin neck and kept swallowing on it.

There were five markers now on the knoll. The dead in the valley outnumbered the living. The valley receded further this time, because not many wanted to think about it. There had been too many deaths in the valley. Particularly in the span of five years and one of the deaths having been bad. And out of Mat having died by snake bite. There had always been snakes in the district, but not many tigers. If you saw a black snake or a brown snake, you got a stick and killed it. They had mostly been taken for granted and you didn't worry about them. Nobody could be remembered as having died by snake bite before.

Mathew Grey had died by snake bite and suddenly everybody felt vulnerable. If a child had gone to play in a paddock, and was late getting home, there would be worry that it might have been bitten by a snake. It concentrated minds on the markers on the knoll. There had been a girl child there, for over seventy years; if she had lived there could have been a family in the valley. She could have mothered a new Grey family.

Old Alec had gone as much from sight as though the valley might have folded in over him.

Another rumour started, it must have come from someone imaginative. The valley had been a sacred place and had been cursed by the Aboriginals. The rumour took hold, as anything with superstition in it can take hold. One of the school teachers took it up, in order to lecture others.

An escarpment of hills, an outbreak of boulders, land that seemed to have nothing on it other than land, perhaps a few trees without visible importance, could be sacred to the Aboriginals. Those inert features could have a mind for the blackmen, more than a mind, a spirit. It could have a spirit in it, the way they had a spirit in them. It could be custodian to their Dreamtime, in the time of the first Gods, in the time of Great Snake and Mother Emu. In the time of the first law givers of totem and taboo.

The Dreamtime spirits had made the earth and everything on it. Everything that came up out of it, everything that walked and slithered over it, every tiny and big thing

108

alive in the earth and on it, and every bird that took wing over it.

The Aboriginals, the first men, could hear the earth and rocks breathing. They could hear the heartbeats in it. They felt and heard the heartbeats and knew it to be so. Although they wore flesh, instead of trees and rocks and water and grass and hills, and flats and valleys, their flesh was of the earth and the earth was of their flesh. The difference was in the form they had assumed. That difference was the same, it had always been the same, always would be, because it could be nothing else having been born of the same mother.

If Grey's valley had been an Aboriginal place, they would have known about the spring, the way the worst drought never altered its bubbling by a pint, they would have known about the shelter there and the migrations of birds. The valley might have had yams in the old days. The Aboriginals had been nomadic, they had never learned to plant a seed. The tribes had kept their water holes secret from each other. Water was as much life and death to them as game to spear, yam patches to find, bushes with berries on them.

Grey's valley could have been sacred. It could have had a curse on it. If it had been a part of the Dreamtime, it could have had a dreaming of its own. It might have had a purpose in it forever. Its purpose could have been to wait on the first Alec Grey, and the purpose that had been in him. To have two men and two women, one a girl child, buried in it to suck. To give the first Grey and his twin sons everything in it. To let them swell on purpose and pride, and then take it away. Take it away bit by bit, and leave nothing in the end.

The first Alec Grey might have known that. He might have known what the end would be, out of the communing he had with the valley. He might have heard the valley breathe, and heard the heartbeats in it. He might have heard the valley thinking, and had known what it would do.

He might have known that there were seeds in the valley he had never planted.

You couldn't look out of a car any more and see the valley. You couldn't get to it unless you knew the way on the back roads. You couldn't see that it was full to bursting with the first Alec's making and everything that had been added by the twins. You couldn't see, and wouldn't have known, that something had come over the valley. The great apple orchard, the smaller one of citrus, the acres where crops had grown, even the outbuildings, were falling into neglect.

The crews talked about it, when they came in. It seemed that nothing was being done between seasons. There were hundreds of dead and dying trees in the orchards. You had to keep up with old orchards like that, root out the dead trees, get new ones in.

The nursery where the new plantings were reared, kept there until they were tall enough and strong enough to be dug into the orchards, the nursery had become neglected. A man had been coming out of Warrawang for years, to do a few months in the nursery. He had been an old codger and had given up. Alec hadn't replaced him or tried to do the work himself.

Old Alec had dropped his bundle, it was hard to believe. When Mat was alive you could think that the orchard, everything in the valley, had been a kind of altar to the twins. The way everything had been maintained, you could think that the valley had been a place of worship. It disturbed the men, some of whom had been working the valley for longer than they cared to remember. So much so that they had come to take a pride in it.

They said that they missed Mat. Mat had always been the easy one to get along with. He would stop for a yarn and a bit of a joke. They remembered when the boy was born, the twins had put on a keg. Mat had come out of the house with a basket, never letting on what was in it. He wouldn't have thought, after all those years in the orchard, that he would

110

be done in by tiger snakes. They intended to keep an eye out for tigers. If they saw one it would get the axe.

The boy wasn't as shy as he used to be. Now he had a need to talk. He would get his own basket and pick for it. He would ride about on his pony trying the help. He would call attention to his snake-proof boots and the snake-proof trousers he wore. They were called snake-proof trousers because there were nobs in the weaving. If a snake tried to bite through the trousers it was supposed to get its fangs tangled in the nobs.

The area with the long hut on it, where the prunings were dried and burned, wasn't far from the knoll and the granite markers. One of the men had gone from the hutments to the run of the spring to do his washing. He saw the boy ride his pony to the knoll and watched him because he had the reins in his teeth and both arms full. The man squatted there with his shirts in the creek and tried to see what the boy was doing. He was doing something at the graves, taking a long time at it. When the boy had got back on his pony the worker had left the creek and gone to the knoll.

On the five graves with their five markers, there were five bunches of flowers. The stems of the flowers were bound with twine. The long end of each of the knots had been put through a cut square of cardboard. It was hard to read the writing on the cards. The writing straggled on the scissored cardboard and had little connection with spelling. When it was puzzled out, the cards read I LOVE YOU.

It was Mick Grimes who told others that old Alec Grey was drinking. It had shocked him when he went to the box with supplies, to read the note with the next order on it. Once a month there would be an order for a dozen bottles of whisky. Nothing other than port had gone to the house, a few glasses of port in the cause of hospitality. The workers remarked on it after that. They would see old Alec outside the house and see that he had two sheets in the wind. You couldn't blame him, the way things had been. Or the way things were now, with just him and the boy in the house. He was too old and too set in his ways to get help. He and his brother had done for themselves and the boy. He'd have a job getting a housekeeper, if he wanted one. No woman they knew, no matter how solitary and hard up, would go out there to look after an old man and a handicapped boy. If she did, the first time she went to the tool shed and saw the scythe, if it hadn't been got rid of, she would be likely to take off screaming.

The thing to wonder about was what would happen to the boy. Everything in the valley was being neglected and old Alec was drinking. He wouldn't live forever. The boy couldn't run the valley. He couldn't run himself. Alec could sell the valley, there would be a fortune in it. But what would happen to the boy without him? No matter how much money he might be left, what would the boy know about money or how to look after himself? When you thought about it you could understand why old Alec Grey was drinking. He might have had something in mind, some provision he had made for the boy so that he could always be looked after.

If Alec sold the valley, what with the money in the bank, he'd be a bloody millionaire. He could take the boy on a world trip. That wasn't likely, since he had hardly ever been out of the valley. He wouldn't know what a ship or an ocean looked like. The boy would probably have a fit, if he was taken out of the valley. When these matters were raised and asked, the valley became a haunt again. Never mind about the ghost of the first Alec Grey being seen at the convict bridge. You'd have thought that if there was going to be a ghost, it would be the ghost of Mat's wife. When a terrible thing like that happened you could get a ghost.

None of that changed old Alec drinking whisky, neglecting the valley and being two sheets in the wind, or that poor little bugger of a handicapped boy, having nobody else in the world. Riding about on his pony, trying to help, and showing you his snake-proof boots and trousers. And taking flowers and messages to put on the Grey's family graves. You could believe the story about the blacks putting a curse on the valley.

Old Alec did take an interest from time to time, but it seemed to be a moody one. He would call one of the men into the house and ask him questions. That had never been done before, asking one of the men into the house. The men would find it difficult to answer old Alec's questions, because of their curiosity about the inside of the house. They would be trying to take in everything they saw. The old tin-type, the furniture, the big case of books, the willow rocking chair with an antimacassar on it, the doors that let off the big room.

Alec would ask them questions they could not answer. Such as were the moss and the weeds being cleared from around the rise of the spring. Was the marsh there getting bigger, and what were they doing about it. Was it black duck, or teal, or wood duck, that had come in that season. Old Alec would have a drink, but he would not offer one.

He would say, 'Truly God is not mocked.' Which didn't mean anything to anyone.

Both the twins had been six feet, or over. Old Alec seemed to be shrinking. He didn't seem to be as tall and he was getting a gut on him. He and Mathew had never had a gut; you could see the meat and the muscle, but it hadn't been a gut. Old Alec had a gut now, it looked spongy when he sat down. The cheeks above the beard, the flesh under the eyes, were plumping and looking unhealthy. The eyes which nobody could ever miss had lost the startling white of their surrounds. The whites looked murky and the icy clarity of the pupils looked murky.

He would say, 'Truly God is not mocked.'

When it had first happened, old Alec asking a man in, it had been regarded as a privilege. Something to tell others, with a distinction for the man invited. That soon passed, with Alec asking questions about what was being done, which had nothing to do with the worker. And telling him,

113

'Truly God is not mocked,' which was disturbing because it was not understood and old Alec must have been drunk and rambling.

Sometimes the boy would be in the room, while Old Alec was rambling. He would put a hand on his shoulder and say, 'Are you tired, Dear One?'

Old Alec's beard had long been grey, now it was going white. He had white in his eyebrows, and his hair had grizzled with grey and white. You could see from the outside that the old house was falling into neglect. If you looked up, in the big room, you could see cracks of daylight. That was something else for heads to be shaken about. The verandah needed re-boarding, you only had to walk on it to know that. Some of the outbuildings had begun to lean and you couldn't trust the doors.

If the valley was falling into neglect, something could have been done about that. There were other things happening further out, which nothing could be done about. There had been a drought for three years. Properties had been burning up and drying away, out on the plains. Wheat farmers, graziers and cocky farmers were being ruined. In Bathurst sale yards you could buy a pen of sheep for twenty pounds, and useful stock horses for ten shillings. In some places, rabbits in hundreds had been seen around the last puddle of muddy water. Rabbits had been seen around the puddles cannibalising other rabbit bodies.

You could smell the stink of death out on the plains, see the dead sheep that had bloated and burst, opened up by the hawks and crows, teeth and tongue protruding from the heads no more now than grotesque masks of themselves. And cattle in the same shape, fed by hand, like the sheep, until the money for bought fodder ran out, and even if it had not, the stock couldn't live without water.

Bitterness arose about Grey's valley, because what was happening there was man-made and not an act of God. The contractor, the selling agent in Sydney, more men than ever needed work. Stockmen, fence builders and dam

114

sinkers could not get work. Neither could the shearers, you can't shear dead sheep.

Men who had never heard of the valley before, heard about it now, because it was said that drought never touched it. Because it was said that the old man who owned it was letting it fall into neglect. He was rich and didn't care that it might have been a Godsend to the many who were up against it, if they could have got a few weeks, or a few months work in that valley.

The place that drought never touched, the place that was bulging in riches, the place that was falling apart and the owner would not employ men to fix it – many of whom would have worked for their keep by then – got heard about to Mudgee, further out to Parkes and Molong and Bogan's Gate, and further out to Trundle, and further out. That was where the drought had hit hardest, and the unemployed had to hear about a place like that. Some could not believe that there could be such a place. They didn't know where it was, but some of the itinerants said they knew about it. They said it was all true, and that stories went with it.

They said that a bush story about a Big Alec, had come out of there. That Big Alec had founded the valley, almost a hundred years ago. He had been the Big Alec in the bush story. In the story Big Alec had jumped a river, with a single-furrow plough in each hand. He had eaten the snooker balls off the table in Moree, or wherever it was being told. He had eaten the snooker balls in mistake for hundreds and thousands. He had picked his teeth with telephone poles and could blow back a gale.

Sometimes the river he had jumped with the plough in each hand had been the Lachlan or the Condamine. Sometimes he had eaten the snooker balls off the table in Walgett, or Come-by-Chance. But the Big Alec in the bush story had been the one who had found the valley. He could lift a laden waggon with one hand. There was an old convict bridge near the valley, and his ghost could be seen there, lifting a waggon or reading the Bible.

The men knew that there wasn't much truth in bush stories, but they were good to tell. In that drought, when it was hard to stay alive, to know where your next feed might come from, it was hard for a man to hear about a place like that, where there was work and you couldn't get it.

If it was true, with a rich man in it, and he wouldn't give a battler work, just sat there letting riches go to pieces, in the worst drought in thirty years, they only hoped that he would fall down and die. You could only put a curse on a man like that.

It was forgotten when the drought lifted. Some remembered that Big Alec had been said to have come from a valley, back in the foothills of the mountains. The bush story about Big Alec survived; the bitterness, if there was such a valley, did not. If the blacks had put a curse on the valley, and another curse on the drought when men had reason to curse, it could make you wonder.

In the next years there were only desultory repairs to the old house and the scatter of buildings around it. The contractor said that he couldn't get through to old Alec. What was done in the seasons was done out of habit. The contractor couldn't give orders about maintenance in the apples and citrus. He couldn't order that old trees must be rooted out. Even if he had, there was nothing in the nurseries to replace them. All he could do was witness it. The stock and station agent did something about the flock. There had been no crutching or earmarking in the new lambs. The flock had gone wild, foraging for themselves. There had always been grass enough, clear water in the run of the spring. Some of the sheep had suffered from unattended fly strike. They were miserable and gone in the hind legs.

The stables had fallen into disrepair. The dray horses and the saddle horses, the grey gelding for the sulky, foraged for themselves on the leavings of the corn crop which had not been reaped. There was no more grain in the feed shed. The stock and station agent had made old Alec an offer for the flock. Old Alec had acepted the offer and told him, 'Truly, God is not mocked.'

Old Alec took an interest in the next harvesting. He would ride up the valley to watch, the boy with him on his pony. Alec would look about him, as though he was seeing it all for the first time. The men would hear the boy say to his uncle, 'Are you tired, Dear One?'

That was the harvest when the boy's cough was more noticed. He would rasp and cough and swallow on his Adam's apple. It wasn't a cough for a handkerchief, it was as dry as spitting sparks. Sometimes he would put his hand on his chest and bend his head. He was a tall boy now, but he had never put on meat. His hands appeared pale enough to see through. When he started the cough you had to see his eyes. Blue eyes as his mother's had been, but as hot and burning as coals. It had always been hard to look at the eyes the Greys had in them, because they seemed to go right through you. If you could hold them, you would think that you were seeing into the backs of their heads. The boy's eyes were not like that. After he had been in a coughing spasm, they burned like blue embers. His thin shoulders would crouch and he would bend on his pony.

Old Alec gave the impression of being lost, in the valley which had been all his knowing. It could be seen that he didn't sit his horse properly, when he rode out. Sometimes he would seem to be two sheets in the wind, sometimes it would seem that he was not there at all, that he was gone away in some other country. He had more than dropped his bundle. He was like someone who did not have a bundle to drop. In some of the crews that came in, those who had been doing it for years, they could be difficult for others to talk to, when they saw old Alec and the boy. If they were picking they jerked at the apples. If a remark was made by a new man, they would tell him to shut up.

At a guess, Alec had to be over seventy. At a guess, the boy would have to be sixteen or seventeen now. He couldn't

117

stop coughing. The old hands had said that the boy had found it hard to talk when he was younger. That he would make words with no words in them. The boy was handicapped. From what the new hands could hear, he could make words enough. He could call old Alec Dear One and ask if he was tired.

Not much is known about what happened next. With old Alec well into his seventies and the boy going on twenty. And going on more than that, going on six feet in height and looking as though he did not have enough meat on him to support it. And for years now hearing his coughing. The doctor's car was often seen in the valley. Old Alec and the boy had been seen at the hospital, driving the sulky to get there, because it was much too late for old Alec to learn to drive a car.

Another thing was known and that caused comment. The old station master, Chadwick, had been replaced. The new one, who had to freight the Grey's produce, sold old Alec two tickets to Sydney. That had to be commented about, a Grey going to Sydney. Mick Grimes had driven them in, there had been a note for him in the box at the entry to the valley. When old Alec and the boy returned, Alec had asked the new station master to telephone Mick Grimes. There was a telephone at the railway station and another in the Railway Arms. Mick Grimes had no telephone, but he had two bowsers now and it wasn't far to his garage to deliver a message. Mick's old Buick had collapsed, he drove a Chevrolet. He arrived at the station and collected old Alec and the boy. The boy had been dressed in a new suit and carried with him large packages, wrapped in striped paper.

The boy, going on a man, had chatted all the way back about what he had seen in Sydney. They had stayed in a hotel, the hotel was huge. When you went to eat there others were eating. It had all been in a big room, the biggest room ever. When you were eating, people brought food to the table. There was water in Sydney, big enough to

118

have boats on it. You could get in the boats and float on the water. Had Mick ever seen a boat that could float on water? A boat full of people, with water to float on? He had been frightened at first. There were things called trams in the streets. Dear One hadn't known what to do at first. A man from Dear One's bank, like the bank in Warrawang, had sent someone to help them. He had never seen anything like that. He had seen a lot of doctors. They must have been friends of Dear One's.

The only thing old Alec had said was, 'Get me back to the valley.'

Mick Grimes went to the Railway Arms. He did not go to The Coronation, which was a new hotel built in the town. He said that he had got old Alec Grey and the boy from the railway station. The boy hadn't stopped talking about trains and trams and boats, and the water in Sydney. There was something wrong with the boy. He had talked about doctors in Sydney.

Mick said that he had known Mat's boy over the years. He could remember when you couldn't make out what he was saying. He had been talking good enough in the car. Words you could understand had been spewing out of him. If old Alec had left the valley to get to Sydney at last, the first time anyone had known him to move, it didn't seem a fair crack of the whip if the boy could make sense now and had to be taken to Sydney to doctors.

Old Alec hadn't said anything. He had worn a new hat. He had just sat in the back, looking out the window. He had looked a bit like he had on the night Mick had driven him back, with Mat's body in a blanket.

All old Alec had said was, 'Get me back to the valley.'

After that visit to Sydney there was nothing that could be done with old Alec. Jim Kearns, the bank manager, who had replaced the first one, Mitchell, had been himself replaced by a new one, Bertie Chivvers. Chivvers was sullen in temper, and had got a bad knee out of athletics. It was said that he had been in a war, it hadn't improved his

119

temper. He had no interest in the valley, but he had inherited the Grey's account.

The contractor had a meeting with him. After twenty-five years of knowing the twins, knowing the second Mary Grey, knowing what had happened to her, knowing how her touch had seemed to make the old house different, this wasn't financial interest. It was out of having to see a place die, out of despair and neglect. Waiting for the last old man to die, with only the handicapped boy left.

The contractor suggested to Chivvers, since he ran the banking, couldn't he prevail on old Alec to sign a paper so that the bank could manage the property. Keep it alive. Up to sixty or seventy men, in the seasons, not to mention their families, partly depended on work in the valley.

Chivvers said he would think about it. He knew nothing about Grey's valley, only the size of the bank account. He wasn't much interested in that, because he intended to take up an interest in the preservation of rain forests. He had had enough trouble in the war he had been to, to say nothing of the limp he had got when he had been an athlete and twisted his knee out of shape. His father-in-law had got him the job in the bank, and the sooner he got out of it the better. However, since it appeared to be a cause of concern, he would drive out and speak to Alec Grey about a paper, if someone would tell him how to get there.

The contractor visited the bank that afternoon and was shown to the manager's office. He asked Chivvers if he had got a paper. How was old Alec? Chivvers was different, after having been to the valley. He had been patronising and resentful about the town. He had made it clear that after three months, he couldn't get out of Warrawang soon enough.

He asked the contractor, 'How long have you known old man Grey?'

'Twenty-five years, he and his twin.'

Chivvers had not known that Alec Grey had a twin.

'Where is the twin?' he asked.

120

'Dead. He died by snake bite. His name was Mathew.'

'What happened to Alec Grey's wife? I met the son.'

'That's Mat's son. Mat's wife died some years back.'

Chivvers said, 'There was nobody at home, when I got there. I went for a walk. I've never seen anything like it. It's hard to believe. It's like something out of a romance novel. Have you seen that old house? It's as much like a fort as a house. Those great granite blocks. The red painted boards on the top of the stone.'

'Not painted red,' the contractor said. 'That's old cedar.'

'That orchard. I've seen orchards. An orchard might go for a few hundred yards. That one must go for a mile. On the slope it's on, looking up, the orchard goes on forever. Those orange and lemon trees. That big rose garden. There are waggons and carts in a shed, they should be in a museum. There's a sulky in a shed. I haven't seen a sulky since I was a boy. I couldn't see a car and thought that Mr Grey must be away. I was leaving when I saw him walking back with his son.'

'His brother's son,' the contractor said, wanting to get down to business. 'Did you speak to Alec about letting the bank manage the property?'

'There's a creek,' Chivvers said. 'The water in it is as clear as crystal. I've seen creeks, they're almost always muddy. The creek is as clear as crystal. I tasted it. I've never drunk water like that.'

'What did Alec say? Did he give you a hearing?'

'There are chooks everywhere. And bantams. I've seen bantams. I've never seen bantams in colours like those. Some of the cock bantams are works of art. Where did they come from?'

'The bantams have been there for years. The twins' father liked bantams.'

'There must be hundreds of them. There's a graveyard not far from the house. I was going to take a look at it when I saw Mr Grey and the young man. The headstones must be four feet high. I was going to take a look at them.'

'Look here,' the contractor said. 'Did you speak to old Alec about letting the bank run the property? That valley's going to rack and ruin. You don't have to tell me what's in it. I've known that valley twenty-five years. Did you talk business, or were you being a bloody tourist?'

'You should see the furniture,' Chivvers said. 'You can see it's all hand made. It should be in a museum.'

'For God's sake,' the contractor said. 'Did you talk business, or didn't you? I can't bugger about all day.'

'He wouldn't talk.'

'Nothing? He wouldn't listen?'

'Oh, he listened. He gave me a drink and wanted to know what Jim Kearns was doing now.'

The other man leaned over the desk and spaced his words.

'Did ... you ... talk ... business?'

'All I could get out of him was that God's will be done.'

'Pour me a drink,' the contractor said. 'I know you've got a bottle in the drawer.'

'The birds,' Chivvers said. 'I've never seen so many birds. There were bird calls coming from everywhere.'

'My God,' the contractor said, and swallowed his whisky, 'I'm glad I don't bank with your mob. That's all old Alec would say?'

'God's will be done.'

'Surely he said something else. If he didn't like the proposition, he must have said so. He must have argued the point about it.'

'God's will be done. That's all. He wasn't offended, he listened. And by the way, let me tell you, it wasn't easy for me. You persuaded me to go out there, so don't get snotty about it. I didn't know I was going to a place like that. I didn't know about Mr Grey. He's like something biblical. There was a big Bible on the table. Everything out there is like another world. He doesn't want to know about the bank managing the place. You persuaded me to go out there. I don't want to manage a property. I don't know how you talked me into it. You get a bloody paper, if you've known the place twenty-five years. One thing's for sure. I'm going back. I'll go to the top of the valley this time. It's all like something out of another world.'

That was the first and last attempt to do something about old Alec having dropped his bundle. The contractor had done well out of the valley for twenty-five years. When he had tried to do something about the neglect, it had not been a selfish interest. The neglect was painful to him. When you remembered the way it had been, the way it was now, the way it would be, it could give any decent man pain.

Bertie Chivvers, only three months in Warrawang, and knowing nothing about Grey's valley, called his clerk to bring him everything relating to the Greys. He had missed the briefing Kearns would have given him. Chivvers had arrived two days after the appointed date. He did not take banking seriously. This was a fill-in occupation, insisted on by his father-in-law, who was a director of the bank. He went through every Grey record, back to the first Grey, when the branch had been founded. He kept saying to himself, 'Blimey!'

He asked his head teller, who had been in Warrawang long enough to know some of the stories. He learned how the young man's mother had died, how his father had been poisoned by tiger snakes. Old Doctor Miskell was semi-retired, he had two locums in the practice. Chivvers made a social arrangement with old Doctor Miskell and heard more stories. He couldn't hear enough about the valley. He began writing down everything he heard. He spoke to the wife of the owner of the Railway Arms, the one who had got the school inspector out to the valley years ago, and wrote that down.

When the stock and station agent was next in town, Chivvers questioned him. He wrote down everything he could learn. He intended to put it into a book. He wrote down the ghost story, and how the blacks had cursed the valley. He knocked on the doors of the old ones in town and

123

learned about Tom Cosgrove. He heard about Ben Saunders, who had bottomed on old crooked seam, and how the first Greys had nursed him and helped him on his way. He learned from middle-aged women and men about the stories they had told, about the giants in the valley and how they had eaten people, when they were children. They laughed about it, remembering back, and told him how the entrance to the valley had been set with dingo traps.

He learned how the first Grey had come out of England on the ball and chain, or some said that he had in the stories. He learned about the first Mary Grey, who had died out of hard work. He found an old man who had known Tom Cosgrove, who delighted in telling stories he had heard from Tom. He wrote down how the pioneer Grey had been like a great rock, as inflexible as a rock, and terrifyingly righteous.

He heard about the Big Alec who had jumped the rivers with a plough in each hand, and had eaten snooker balls off the table, and how he had picked his teeth with telephone posts and could blow back a gale.

If the valley was in neglect, so was Chivvers' attention to banking. He had fancied he could write, from time to time, but had nothing to write about. Now he had a subject. He would write about the Greys and the valley. He sent a letter to Kearns, who was being important at head office. Kearns answered him, he was interested and put everything he knew in the exchange of letters.

Kearns told Chivvers how he had looked in the family Bible, when he had gone to the valley for a burial. The Bible had come from England and it had births in it going back generations. And told him that there had been no entry for an Alec Hannibal Grey. There had been other Hannibal Greys in the Bible, back four generations. Kearns told Chivvers in a letter, that when he had first looked in the Bible, there was something inside the cover that could have been a coat of arms.

This correspondence continued for a year. Kearns wrote

Chivvers an account of how he had advertised for a wife for Mat, that old Alec had come in on the fiftieth birthday of the twins, and had said that they needed a son for the valley. A son to look to the valley when he and his brother were gone.

Most of the executive work in the bank was being done by the head teller. He was glad to do it, seeing himself as the next manager. The present manager became irritable if he had to concentrate on banking. He spent every day and all day writing a book about something.

For two years Bertie Chivvers wrote about Grey's valley. He must have had an instinct for research, and sent to Sydney for a back-date on the story that had been in a magazine, with photographs in it. He learned from Mick Grimes that the son was handicapped, and how his uncle had taken him to Sydney to see doctors. He wrote notes about the stand of cedar, and the marsh where the spring got up, and how migrating birds never failed to get there.

For two years he put the stories together, becoming a joke in the town, because he could never hear enough. When the contractor returned for harvesting, Chivvers and his wife had him to dinner night after night.

He came in now a month before the crews. He would go out to the valley to see that it was prepared. Two men with him to help, a lot had to be done. The hutments on the burning flat had to be repaired. Apple boxes had to be repaired, new ones got. New baskets had to be got. New straw palliasses had to be got, the old ones burned. Paint and stencils were needed to put on the boxes. The apple waggons and apple drays were no longer used. The harness for them was falling to pieces, everything was motorised. The contractor had not got the paper he had wanted. He did it his way, and put it on the bill. When he told old Alec what he was doing, Alec had done no more than nod.

He had said, 'One old man and a boy in Grey's valley, now.'

The contractor's men would hammer at new ladders. He

would go into town and order beef and mutton. The flock had been sold, there was nothing left for slaughter. He would order flour, salt, tea, sugar. Potatoes and carrots and any fresh vegetables in season. If their keep wasn't there, that was in their contracts, the men would strike. You couldn't let that happen, with almost four thousand trees to harvest. Which had to be done when the fruit was early ripe, so that it would arrive crisp and crunchy in the markets.

All that would be put on the Grey account at the shops. The bank manager would pay that, and any other account. If it had been left to old Alec, nothing would have been done.

Old Alec knew what was happening. He had been told about it. He had nodded agreement and said, 'God's will be done.'

Bertie Chivvers would be in the valley at pruning and harvesting. When the men stopped work to eat, he would be among them. He would ask for how long had they been going to the valley. What could they remember of Mathew Grey. Had any of them been there when his wife had died. Could any of them remember when the boy had been born. Had they heard about the curse that had been put on the valley.

Those who knew the valley well had nothing to risk with a bank manager, mostly having no money in any bank. They didn't like the questions, when they were taking a break. They put up with it for a time. Then they told Chivvers to bugger off. He did not bugger off, he would leave those men and go to others. They would tell him to bugger off. The contractor had to speak to him.

'Leave the men alone,' he said. 'I'm not against what you're doing. I hope you make a good fist of it. It's a story worth the telling. These are good men, but rough. If you keep getting up their noses like that, one of them will bend yours. These men are battlers. They've had to live a way you would never know. They don't care that you're a bank

manager. To them you're a bloody sticky-beak. I've told
you before, I'll tell you again. I'm glad I don't bank with
your mob. For Christ's sake, Bertie, stay in your bank and
do banking.'

Chivvers kept it up, in those years. He was industrious
about it and his wife helped him. He began his book with
the first Alec Grey taking ship out of Liverpool. He had a
brass-bound tool box with him and apple seeds in a leather
pouch. There were still convicts then. He didn't let that
disturb him. He helped build the troubled young city, on
the blue water, among the gum trees. When he had saved
enough he married. He took a dray and four pack-horses.
He crossed the Blue Mountains on the track the explorers
had found. The first Alec Grey had stopped at a hump-
backed bridge, built by the convicts. He saw the entrance to
the valley, because he had been waiting on it.

That was the beginning of the book Chivvers wrote. He
put a lot in the book, after that beginning. He spoke to
Doctor Miskell again, about Alec's health and his nephew's
health. He had got to know the young man, having sought
him out when he was getting material from the men, or not
getting material when he irritated them. A mind that had
never fully developed was sad to see in the child, sad to see
in the boy. It was sadder, much sadder, in a young man six
feet tall. Chivvers became interested in old Alec's health,
because young Alec had not another soul in the world,
other than his Dear One. He continued to call him that in
his twenties. Nobody had ever heard him use uncle.
Chivvers was looking ahead, in the book he was writing.

The idea that old Alec must have made a provision for
the boy, somewhere in a home where he could be looked
after all his life, was not in any paper the bank held. Both
twins had recorded wills to be held by the bank. There had
been wills before Mary died, leaving her and the boy
everything. New wills after that, leaving everything to the
boy, both the twins half shares in everything, to go to the
boy, if one died before the other.

Doctor Miskell told Chivvers that the boy had tuberculosis. He had referred old Alec to specialists in Sydney, which was why he had gone there. Miskell had thought that a sanitarium of which there were a number high in the Blue Mountains, where the air was believed to be beneficial, might effect a cure, or at least a mending. The specialists in Sydney had taken X-rays. Young Alec's situation was hopeless, both lungs were scarred. It was an unusual case. It was so bad it might be thought he had been born with the disease. Old Alec had brought back sealed letters to show Miskell.

The old man must have been in agony at that news. The last of the Greys, the heir to the valley, had not only been born retarded, he did not have long to live. God's will be done. Young Alec Hannibal's Dear One must have been living his days and nights in an agony of the spirit. It must have been an agony for him to look at the valley, let alone do anything in it. To listen to anyone about anything, with an agony like that inside him. He might have found something in the Bible to comfort him. Even though I walk in the valley of the shadow of death, his father's prayer over graves, his own and Mathew's when Mary was buried, Alec's when he buried his twin, could have been a mockery now. In everything that valley had seen and known, old Alec might have cursed the God he had lived by. That had happened in other men for lesser reason.

It hadn't happened in old Alec. He had said, 'God's will be done.' He had said, 'Truly God is not mocked.'

Young Alec had a horse to ride, when he went up the valley to be with the men. He had long outgrown the pony. He had been lengthening his stirrups for years. His snake-proof trousers had lengthened, so had his snake-proof boots. So had his spasms of coughing.

Old Alec had employed a man to live in the hutments. He gave him no work to do. He had employed him to be there. The man had been on the track and had gone to the house for a handout. He had driven the sulky to get Doctor

Miskell. Old Alec was nursing the boy. He had got a cold, the cold had got something else. Old Alec must have been waiting for it. Doctor Miskell didn't send one of his locums. He drove out himself. He and old Alec put the boy in the car, to be driven to the hospital. Miskell told Chivvers that he had been sinking then. Old Alec had held his hand, long after he had been made comfortable on the back seat of the car, with a pillow for his head and a blanket over him. Miskell had gone to the back of the car, old Alec standing at the open door. He had spoken as gently as he could, old Alec had not appeared to hear. His great hand was holding the pale hand of young Alec. Miskell had gently broken the grip. He had looked back once. Old Alec had not moved, he was standing there holding out the hand that had held the hand of young Alec.

Alec Hannibal died in the hospital, after five days. In that time his uncle had not visited. Young Alec had contracted pleurisy. What was left of his lungs soon succumbed. He had peacefully died, in coma.

When he was brought back from the hospital the hired hand had a grave dug. There was a cedar coffin ready, it might have been ready for years. Doctor Miskell was there, a new Church of England minister, and Chivvers, from the bank. When the service was over, old Alec walked away. He had not said a word since he had been brought from the house. He did one thing, which could have been words. He bunched his great fist and shook it at the sky. He turned and shook the fist, looking up the valley to the cedars. Then he had seemed to collapse, or bend over, as one can at a bad stomach pain. Then he had shambled back to the house.

The new minister had asked Miskell should they go with him. Miskell had shaken his head. The old doctor had tears in his eyes.

'No,' he had said. 'There is nobody to go with.'

There was only one old man in the valley. Mick Grimes continued to deliver supplies, judging for himself what might be needed. He had not been getting orders in the box. He would get a few things together, and once a month deliver a dozen bottles of whisky.

Chivvers wrote it all down, at last he didn't have to put in his research something got by hearsay. Two years after the death of Alec Hannibal, old Alec got in the sulky and drove to the bank. He knew which days the solictor was in Warrawang. The solicitor was young, had done law, taken over from his father. Alec asked Chivvers to send for him. He sat with his eyes shut, while he waited. It was a long wait. Chivvers left his office and found something to do with the tellers. He couldn't sit across a desk with a man who had nothing to say, who sat there with his eyes shut.

The legal meeting was a long one. The son of the father the Greys had known for years, awed to meet a Grey, because his father had often spoken about them, and about Grey's valley, became confused and uncertain. Old Alec told him to get it all down. If he couldn't do it, his father would put it to rights. Chivvers became uncertain and confused. Old Alec would lay his eyes on them both, he had no confusion in him. He asked the young man if he knew anything in law to contradict his intention. The young man didn't know, he didn't think so. Old Alec told him to take it up with his father. The young man said it would have to be researched.

Old Alec said, 'When you have the papers ready, bring them to me to sign. You come with him,' he said pointing at Chivvers.

The young man said, 'If it can be done, Sir, it will have to be done through a trust.'

'I have no concern how it is done,' old Alec told him, 'I am concerned that it should be done. I am concerned that there must not be a loophole in it. I am concerned that it must be done now. Talk it over with your father.'

He left then. Chivvers and the young man, who had not long been a lawyer, were left to stare at each other. Chivvers got the whisky out.

He said, 'I've never heard of anything like this. Will it hold up in law?'

130

'I will have to get advice. I've never heard about anything like this.'

'Talk to your father,' Chivvers said, who didn't know about a father, and had not known about his son.

'Why would he want to do it?' the young man asked.

'I've got an idea about it,' Chivvers said. 'I've been making notes about the Greys, to stop me going mad in this hell hole. I'm going to write a book about the valley. I didn't expect to have this drop into my lap. Have you ever seen the valley and the old house? I was out there when the son was buried. I had a good look at the headstones. Do you know what's on the first Grey's headstone? Just his name and the dates. Below that, HE CAME HERE.'

'Just that? He came here?'

'That's all. There's a headstone for a little girl, going back to blazes. There's nothing on that one, just the name and the dates.'

'Do you think that Mr Grey mightn't be competent? You have to be in sound mind, you know.'

'Did he sound incompetent? He was dismissing things you said. He wouldn't budge an inch. If that old man's incompetent, you and I need treatment. No, this is something I'll have to work out; I'm getting a feeling about it. The thing is, will it hold up in law?'

'I've never heard of a precedent for it. Nothing that even comes close. I'll have to get advice, have it researched.'

Chivvers said, 'Talk it over with your father. He knew the Greys.'

'It's not a matter of knowing anyone. It's a matter of law.'

'When will you be back with the papers?'

'This could take months to research. Even then, it will probably have to go to the bench to be tested.'

'It's like a romance,' Chivvers said. 'You wouldn't believe that old house. You wouldn't believe the valley. I picked up a story that the blacks had cursed it. I picked up a bush yarn about a Big Alec. It's supposed to be about the first Alec Grey.'

'Was that Mr Grey's sulky outside?'

131

'A bit of a wreck, isn't it? I've picked up stories about that, how the twins had never bought a car.'

'You don't often see sulkies these days. Is there as much money in the bank as people say?'

'You wouldn't believe it,' Chivvers said. 'I've been through that account since the first deposit.'

'There would be nothing to stop it, then, if it holds up in law?'

Chivvers said, 'If it holds up, mate, you and I will be dead and gone long before there's anything to stop it.'

For the first time in over one hundred years, in all the stories true and invented, what had passed between old Alec and the others when he went to sit in the bank, was not known in the town. It was too haunting to talk about. There was an awful finality in it.

The papers did come. The young lawyer brought them after three months. His father, who had retired, came to Warrawang before that. He spent an afternoon in the valley, talking to old Alec. A few weeks afterwards he returned, going to the valley to talk again.

He had been well known in the town, many had been glad to see him. His son used the office he had used for so many years. He had been the one with the old bank manager who had looked in the family Bible. Those who met him on those visits said he had changed. He looked well in his retirement, but instead of renewing old acquaintances he had been no more than civil. Tommy Thompson had done many a good turn, in law. He had represented some in litigations who could not pay, and he had known that and had never bothered them. He had come back twice to go from his old office to the valley. If you stopped him on the street, he couldn't be more than civil.

It was said that Alec Grey was selling the valley to a syndicate in Sydney. He had got old Tommy Thompson out of retirement to handle it for him. He wouldn't deal with the son, you could understand that, the son was still wet behind the ears. If old Alec got a million for the valley it

132

wouldn't be much good to him. Talk about his father's ghost haunting the convict bridge. He was no better than a ghost himself, and had been like that for years.

It was a bugger of a business, the way the young 'un had died. There hadn't been much of him from the first, when his father had brought him out in a basket for the men to look at. He hadn't stopped crying, when he was a baby, and the twins used to cart him around. He'd always had one cough and another, when he was a boy riding a pony. He'd always been liked. You had to be sorry for him, being handicapped, but you could forget about that, because young Alec had always been liked for himself. The way he would try to help when the crews were in, offering them a sandwich he had cut for his lunch. Getting all twisted up in the face when he couldn't get his words right, but never complaining, and running messages if a man needed a new basket. There were dozens of saws in the tool shed. If a man needed a new saw at pruning, young Alec would be off on his pony to get it. Or a new axe, if a handle had broken and had to be replaced from the tool shed. Nobody had ever heard young Alec complain, and all the time he had been dying.

Another who could hardly be civil these days, was Hargreaves, the contractor. When he came in to stay at the Railway Arms, which he had been doing in the seasons for as long as could be remembered, if you stopped him on the street to ask about old Alec, or was it true that old Alec had dropped his bundle, he'd get angry enough to hit you. One good thing about a syndicate taking over the valley, what had been let go out there would be fixed up. There would always be work in Grey's valley.

One more harvest passed. Old Alec was not seen. The roses had gone wild and unattended. The fowls and the bantams had gone wild, they had to fend for themselves. The hired hand had gone, he had fed them before. He might have gone because he wanted to. He might have been told to go. There wasn't a horse left, not a grey for the sulky. Old Alec had sold the horses, the way he had sold the sheep. All the birds around the house were as numerous as ever.

Mick Grimes found old Alec, when he had gone to the box with his supplies. His last delivery was in the box and old Alec was stretched out dead. He had died before he could collect his supplies. He had lain there for a fortnight. Or it must have been near that, because Mick made his delivery every two weeks. Mick got the body in the car and drove it to the house. He had hauled old Alec into the house, got the body on the sofa he remembered from when Mat's body had been on it. Mick had helped old Alec to do that. There was nobody to help him and the big body was heavy. Mick shut the door and drove fast into town.

The burial on the knoll was done by others. There was no Grey who could be present, or read from the Bible. In old Alec's will there was an instruction where to put him. Like his father, he had carpentered his own cedar coffin.

If you travel that back road, the first to come down from the mountains, laboured at by convicts who had built the hump-backed bridge, you will see the valley.

Anyone can go there and take anything they want. The old house is ruined and stripped. The apple orchard and the citrus orchard are a tangled ruin. The privet hedges nest more birds than they ever did. They aren't hedges any more, they are wild trees of privet. There's not much left of the house only the granite, only the granite blocks too big to move. The cedar has gone, the cedar beams and the cedar planks are serving use somewhere else.

There isn't much left of the outbuildings. Anything in them, and any good timber, has long gone somewhere else.

Only the spring has not changed. Migrating birds in flocks use the marsh as they had done long before the whitemen. The leaves continue to fall in the apple orchard. They fall feet deep, as do the apples. Visitors taking apples, those who go there to get as many as they can, can't harvest a crop off more than four thousand trees. Small marsupials, everything that can burrow, black snakes, brown snakes and tiger snakes, make a home in the fallen leaves.

Long grass hides the graves on the knoll. The grass is halfway up the markers.

Old Alec provided in his will that it should be so. Nobody can live in the valley, while there is Grey money to pay the rates and taxes.

Nobody else should ever own it, while there is money to see that nobody ever owns it.

Also from Penguin

DAVID FOSTER

Plumbum

Australia and New Zealand proudly present the world's
most notorious rock bank! Plumbum. The ultimate
heavy metal experience.

Dog Rock

Somewhere, in the Australian countryside, a small and
closely knit community harbours a dangerous killer.
Not since *Under Milkwood* has country life been
portrayed with such affection and humour.

The Pure Land

Three generations of a family move restlessly from the
Blue Mountains of New South Wales to the east coast of
the United States and back in search of fulfilment.

The Adventures of Christian Rosy Cross

A comic retelling of the Rosicrucian myth, Foster's
iconoclastic account of his youthful hero's travels in the
East is at once a picaresque fiction, a scholarly
contribution to the history of spiritual alchemy, an ethic
for the drug user and a lament for the now-departed
spirit of the 1960s.

DAVID MALOUF

Johnno

An affectionately outrageous portrait, *Johnno* brilliantly recreates the sleazy tropical half-city that was wartime Brisbane and captures a generation locked in combat with the elusive Australian Dream.

Fly Away Peter

The timeless and idyllic world of the Queensland coast in 1914 contrasts sharply with life in another hemisphere as it rushes headlong into the brutal conflict of war.

Child's Play

In the streets of an ordinary Italian town people go about their everyday lives, while secretly a young man rehearses for his greatest performance. An effective and penetrating study of the mind and being of a fanatic.

Harland's Half Acre

From his poverty-stricken upbringing on a dairy farm in Queensland, Frank Harland nurtures his artistic genius until the time comes when he can take possession of his dreams.

Antipodes

Stories which pinpoint the contrast between the old world and the new, between youth and age, love and hatred and even life and death itself.